WELLTON COUNTY HUNTERS

Wellton County Hunters

A novel

by

SIMON A. SMITH

Adelaide Books
New York / Lisbon
2021

WELLTON COUNTY HUNTERS

A novel

By Simon A. Smith

Published by Adelaide Books, New York / Lisbon
adelaidebooks.org

Editor-in-Chief
Stevan V. Nikolic

For any information, please address Adelaide Books
at info@adelaidebooks.org

or write to:

Adelaide Books
244 Fifth Ave. Suite D27
New York, NY, 10001

ISBN: 978-1-955196-93-2

Printed in the United States of America

1

If Molly could see him now. Naked, vulnerable, up to his neck in Lysol, rubber gloves, and steel wool. The nudity seemed to add another layer of humiliation to the task, but he was going to take a bath anyway, and it wouldn't make sense to ruin a perfectly good shirt or pair of pants… He'd always maintained that he was practical if nothing else. Russ stooped closer to the sash. The flab around his belly folded into a lumpy crease above his waist and just sort of scrunched there. It was hard to ignore the pulpy friction, but he managed it. Lethargy had gotten him into this mess, and it would be lethargy that would get him out. Besides, he was interested in something else. He pressed his eyeball up so close that his lashes grazed the bottom ridge. There, along the base of the window, were what had first appeared to be little bubbles of paint. Upon closer inspection, Russ discovered that the tiny mounds were not pockets of air at all but rather miniscule bugs lacquered over with brown paint. What creeped him out the most was that he could see what he thought were itty-bitty legs and antenna crystalized into hardened dots of exoskeleton. What kind of heartless, sadistic soul would do such a thing? What kind of a maniac would varnish a poor insect to death with a fucking paintbrush? Was it intentional? It made him a little sick to think about it. He couldn't help wondering if his melodramatic response to the demise of such microscopic organisms was due in part to the recent departure of his ex-girlfriend. Perhaps her desertion had caused him more suffering than he'd like to admit. It did strike him as odd that only now, in the face of such curious circumstances, was he able to muster up the type of deep emotions that Molly had been seeking all along. Perhaps this was why she had fled, his failure to produce these same humane sentiments when they were needed the most. Or maybe she left because of the actual insects themselves. Maybe she had spotted them there weeks ago and couldn't recover from the fact that this man, her boyfriend, would just leave them there, ignore them, these helpless creatures, all speckly and crusted over… But things were rarely what they first appeared.

The truth was, the black mold festering along the bottom of the window had been a longstanding bone of contention. Molly claimed he hadn't maintained the space with the proper fastidiousness and that, even after the damage was done, he hadn't scrubbed hard enough with a stiff enough sponge or hadn't washed it with a stringent enough cleaner. Russ's argument was that it was a window inside a bathtub, which made it more susceptible to fungus, and he swore that if he had scrubbed any harder he'd have sanded straight through the entire wall. Not to mention, Russ was quick to point out, the tub and the windows and the whole damn place had been built in like 1940, and nobody had ever taken the time to update or fix a single thing in eighty years. Molly made it sound as if he wanted the mold there, like he had willed it there out of spite, was proud of the stubbornness with which it clung to the edges of glass and wood. What Russ received for this impassioned argument was a broken relationship, general abandonment, a worn leather sofa and one month's rent for the small, grimy apartment they'd been sharing together at 1344 West Slate Street.

Russ removed the yellow rubber gloves and set them on the ledge next to the spray cleaner and furry sponge. He took a seat on the edge of the tub and sighed. Window mold was not the only way in which the couple proved incompatible. As always happened after a time, women became bored with him. Where other men seemed laidback and lighthearted, Russ was serious and contemplative in a way that made women wonder if there might be a more exciting option available. Perhaps there was a man out there, they'd ponder, who would be happy to watch a Superhero movie without commenting on the plausibility of certain action sequences or the incongruity of dialogue by this or that invincible character. Just the notion of invincibility alone seemed so *fucking* puerile to him.

It was hard to go to bed with a man after something like that, Russ knew. He couldn't help himself. If he was being honest, and he'd never really had the chance to be that with any substantial girlfriend, he'd rather sit in the kitchen and discuss, say, the paradox of free will rather than talk about an upcoming music festival or the newest diet trend, which he knew made him a peculiar college boy, especially a Wellton College one. Molly was aware of his quirky pursuits from the start. It wasn't as though he'd ever hidden his interests. She knew he was studying philosophy at Wellton College. It had been part of his nerdy appeal during their initial courtship. Russ's idea of romance was drinking an entire bottle of red wine and discussing Martin Heidegger. In the beginning, he'd either known just enough about pinot noir, or she'd known just too little about it, to make the whole pompous spectacle an enticing affair. That he had dropped out of Wellton one month into his third semester was also part of the deterioration of his eccentric allure. And so, he was never quite shocked when another woman walked out on him, but that didn't make it hurt any less.

Standing, Russ's bare butt cheeks made a crass flatulent sound as they peeled up from the tub's porcelain rim. He cranked the spigot and listened to the water come gushing from the faucet. He raised the blackened window a crack and let the night wind swirl across his naked body. The mixture of hot water and cool breeze always made him feel light and woozy. The joint he had rolled right before getting undressed was still waiting for him by the sink. Because the bathroom was small and cramped, he could reach over and pluck it up without too much contorting. Even with the toilet in between, the distance from sink to tub was still less than five feet or so. There, sitting on the counter next to the joint, was one of the only things Molly had neglected to take with her when she retreated. It was unclear if she'd forgotten the vanilla scented candle in the fancy glass jar by accident or if she had left it behind as a sort of parting gift for a man who could use a little air freshener in his life. Whether or not it was a passive aggressive token of her displeasure, didn't much matter to Russ. He kind of liked it. The fact that nothing else in his entire apartment bore even the slightest resemblance to this decorative and dainty object, brought a smile to his face. It was, after all, with its charming effect, the perfect companion to offset the undesirable chore he had just completed. And so, as he bent down to ignite the spliff on its flickering, aromatic tip, he felt a spreading sense of levity and release. He took a full drag and blew the smoke out through the window. It was cheap weed, harsh and flaky with an abundance of stems and seeds. It was the best one could do in Wellton. It was Valley View chronic, and just like the scenic setting the name implied, the elevated effect was a lie. In the weeks since Molly left, he'd been thinking about his stunted life and all of the ratty things in it. The low-grade pot was just another sign of his stagnant progression into adulthood, same as the hard and frameless mattress, frayed carpets and chipped tiles.

Bob Marley was a part of it, too. From where he stood he could see the red striped edge of a Rasta flag draped over the front door. He'd bought it a number of years ago when the Lion of Judah still held some mystical meaning to him, and songs like "Three Little Birds" seemed to have the power to change the world. He was going to take it down as soon as he was done bathing.

The tub was almost full and with it his lame self-pity. The fog-covered alley outside the window offered no relief. Its backdrop was little more than a steady line of faded garage doors, dented trash cans and discarded dreams. Russ 's long exhale ended in a mournful groan. The vacant landscape was a metaphor for his broken heart. Of the three streetlights, only one was still working, a dull, flickering bulb illuminating nothing more than a broken hairdryer and the rotting remnants of a peaked TV dinner.

Ah, hell... He had to physically slap the wallowing out of his system. It would have worked too, except the spot he'd chosen to strike was the loosened skin around his stomach. It was a sad, fleshy smack, causing Russ to call out in sorrow. He'd grown so pale and tender over the last few months that he could see the pinkish outline of his fingers printed around his belly button. It looked like a grade school drawing, a child's sketch of a hand-turkey for some Thanksgiving art project. The last time he was this out of shape was high school. There had been a concerted effort in college to use his gym pass, run laps and lift weights occasionally. When he was trying to win over Molly, a former field hockey star on her high school team, he'd put in a lot of time at the school's sports facility, but as they grew more comfortable together, so too did the inertia and sluggishness of contentment blooming around him. This was the curse of a long-term relationship. Complacency. Damn it, he thought, I'm going to die old and alone right here in this godforsaken bathtub. Molly was about the only pretty girl left in town, and now he was a college dropout pushing thirty with a doughy gut, a moldy window and the mindset of a drifting stoner from another era. About the only bright spot in his meager existence was the new job he was about to start on Monday morning, but if he was expecting an entry-level position as a bank teller to save him he was even more deluded than he thought. He shut off the water about thirty seconds before it overflowed the sides. He tossed the roach out the window. Shit, it was muggy. Almost November and still sixty-five degrees outside at midnight. Global warming, man. Fuck. The open window may as well have been a slab of insulated stuffing. The whole world was narrowing in on the type of fiery ending only Robert Frost could have predicted.

Calm down, Russ. That's what he told himself. He spoke out loud but in a whisper. Whatever small amount of pride he had left would not allow him to embarrass himself further by having one of his reactionary neighbors overhear his breakdown. What did it matter? He'd never taken the time to get to know his neighbors anyway. He was living on the second floor, sandwiched between the top and bottom stories of the complex, and for a while he considered trying to make friends with a few of the other tenants, but he could never quite get past his fear of intimacy or maybe it was his fear of rejection. A little of both was probably true. Regardless, given time, they'd just end up shunning him and all his dopehead habits anyways.

All right, now… He took a deep breath, let the marijuana take hold and do its trick. You're overreacting, man. Just chill out and relax. You're freaking out. Everything is going to be fiiiiiiine… He grabbed hold of the sides of the wall and began his slow descent into the steaming bath.

It was at the soothing, audible moment when his ass made contact with the suds and the tension sought to drain itself into the water, that he heard a loud popping sound. Before he could scramble back up on his feet he heard another one. It was the boom of a firecracker but with the added weight and volume of intention. Gasping, he slopped his dripping torso up onto the window ledge and peered out. What he saw was a thin figure crumpled on the pavement beneath the one desolate streetlight. In the distance, moving farther afield at a mad pace, he glimpsed a lumbering silhouette fleeing through a cloud of fog and smoke. The perpetrator was larger but not necessarily in height or age. He seemed to carry within his stocky shoulders and clopping stride the heft of anger and experience. But all Russ could really make out, seeing him only from behind as he vanished into the haze, was his bulky black coat and sagging sweatpants. The blast left a ringing behind that still echoed in his ears.

"Jesus Christ!" Russ shouted, no longer concerned with his uptight neighbors. The victim, no more than thirty feet below where Russ stood trembling, was motionless and disheveled in a way that could make a person think it was only a heap of clothing masquerading as a felled human body. A cruel joke. But it wasn't a joke. He was dead.

2

Downtown Wellton was a time capsule from a period of rejuvenation, a postcard from the prosperous years following World War II. The area was still imbued with those returning soldiers, both in ghost form and in the form of hoary shop-keepers like Martin Kestler, the eighty-year-old owner of MK Sporting Goods on Main Street. For decades now Mr. Kestler had been mostly known for carrying baseball cleats from the 1970s and selling Abba Zaba candy bars, which had gone out of business in 1998. One did not have to look far for more Martin Kesslers in the neighborhood. They ran the barbershop on Hill Top Road, owned the gas station in the square and maintained the church grounds over at St. Benedict parish.

Wellton also did its best to pay homage to the frontiersman who settled the area in 1846. Though there was no monument present, the impression of one seemed to always be looming. There was a conjuring that the mind did automatically upon viewing the scenery, an image of a pioneer perched on a hillside dressed in animal pelt boots and coat, satchel and shotgun poised above one shoulder. All part of the rustic charm. After all, many of the residents had ancestry dating all the way back to the Austrians and Germans who forged Wellton into existence, and so they cherished the bucolic, wistful reminders. They insisted upon them. The main street did a fine job granting these wishes. The most recent addition was the renovated movie theater, The Halcyon, which was rumored to have originally been the first home of William Penn's great-grandson. The Marquee was in the shape of an enormous squire hat with a feather on top. The avenue's crowning touch may have been the banner stretched above the central square perpetually advertising whatever celebration or festival was in season. The one spanning the street today read, "Harvestfest" in tall brown and yellow letters with a strand of pumpkins, gourds and cornucopias laced around the border. Russ, having zero connection to the agricultural practices common in this part of Pennsylvania, had no real understanding of the emblem's significance beyond his appreciation for the farm-style beers that he knew were created special for the occasion.

It was this pastoral ambiance that made his new job all the more complicated for him. The thing was that without a doubt one of the most vital and recognized establishments in the entire downtown was the Riegler Community Bank. The structure had been a pillar of the region since 1859. It stood like a grand and stoic mansion on the northwest corner of Main Street. Like the majority of other buildings in the vicinity, it was made of gray quarry stone and built in a solid, indomitable style that seemed to emulate the general disposition of its enduring citizens. It was those citizens and this most symbolic bank before him that Russ was contemplating as he sat inside the RCB parking lot with his 2007 Ford Escort still idling. How had he come to this point, after all of his apprehensions? Here he was about to embed himself, willingly, inside one of the most venerable institutions Wellton had to offer. It was like James Dean going to work for the local bowling alley in Marion, Indiana. To be sure, he was no James Dean, but that was not the point. It was more about the statement this would make. Right above the main entrance hung a huge American flag. The sheer visage of spotless austerity and unquestioned allegiance made Russ gag a little on the final drag of his cigarette. He wasn't sure if he could go through with it, but as he reached into the glove box to find a breath mint and then listened to the sputtering clatter of his car engine as he turned off the ignition, he knew he had no choice.

The first thing the eye was drawn to inside the Riegler Bank was the enormous vault behind the counter. Before Russ could fully orient himself, a familiar man in a pair of high-waisted khakis and a slick comb-over alighted from the steel mouth of the depository as though propelled and bolstered by its promised security. He approached in a friendly but erect and professional manner, offering his hand a good twenty feet before reaching him. Russ accepted his palm and shook it with what he hoped was the right amount of banker-like pressure.

"Dwayne Albright Fischer," the man said.

"Russell Jerome Cooper," Russ said. It had been some time since he'd used his full name like that, which made him stutter a bit, and already he had his first concern of the day. Did bankers always use their entire names when they greeted someone? That would be on his mind all day now.

It seemed odd that they were being so formal. Though they had never officially spoken before, they had been informally acquainted by their mutual attendance at Wellton High School. Russ knew that Wayne had graduated two years ahead of him and was able to recall his routine presence in the hallways. With fewer than four hundred students in the entire building, Russ felt certain he must have been at least partially aware of his tumultuous reputation. By the time Wayne left the school, Russ had already been suspended twice for possession of marijuana and once for public intoxication. That Wayne had gone ahead and hired him despite everything, had filled Russ with a mixture of gratitude and trepidation leading up to this date. Had he taken him on as some sort of reclamation project or out of some latent yearning to teach him and his wayward kind a stiff lesson about servitude?

"Let's get you settled in," Wayne said. "You can put your coat inside our closet over here. Would you like any tea or water?"

"Do you have any coffee?" Russ asked.

Wayne paused. "I think we can rustle some up," Wayne said. "Rustle. Ha! No pun intended."

"None taken," Russ said. The slight hesitation in Wayne's response worried Russ. Had he involuntarily communicated something about his dark leanings through his craving for caffeine?

As they walked together toward the back corner of the floor, Russ couldn't help noticing how clean and sterile everything was. Pressed vacuum lines still ironed the gold carpet, and the brass railings along the countertops were polished and glimmering. From what Russ could tell, he and Wayne were the only ones inside the building so far. He wasn't sure of the total number of workers at the bank, but it couldn't have been many. Physical banks, even in Wellton, were living relics, and everything in the place, from the ornate pillars that stood in the vestibule to the massive wall clock above the exit, seemed to be hinting toward a moment of recession.

For the most part, Wayne looked exactly like he remembered him from high school, still wiry and angular with a jaunty stride and a feckless gaze behind thick glasses. Russ couldn't recall if Wellton High had an accounting club, but if they did no doubt Wayne would have been the president.

"Here we are," Wayne said. "This is our break room, meeting room, coat closet and little general store all rolled into one."

"Sounds good to me," Russ said. As Wayne pushed open the door, Russ caught a glimpse of perhaps the only dusty object in the whole space. Over the entrance there hung a dingy wreath with a faded red bow in the middle. Russ wondered if they had hung it in early anticipation of this year's Christmas or if it had been a bad oversight from last year's holiday season. Neither option made Russ happy.

Unlike the main floor, this room was dank and unkempt. Aside from a small loveseat against the wall and a few ancient appliances scattered about, there wasn't much to it. The lingering smell of ten thousand microwaved lunches was masked beneath many coats of bleach cleaner and unseen mothballs. Russ's jacket was the first one to be draped across the wooden hooks on the coat hanger. Wayne reached for the coffee maker on the counter. His movements were muffled by the giant rumbling refrigerator beside him. Russ was certain the monstrous thing must have been older than Wayne himself.

"Let's see," Wayne said as he slid the coffee maker forward and opened the cabinet overhead. Russ was glad to see that the appliance had clearly been used recently. He wasn't the only coffee drinker here. Perhaps that meant he'd make a friend later. "It's Monday morning. We just opened. In about ten minutes Harold Weber is going to come in to deposit his social security check, followed by Doris Forney who will want to know why her check from the grocery store bounced again."

"Doris is a schemer, huh?" Russ said, hoping for some good gossip.

"No," Wayne said in a somber tone. "She's senile. You have to watch out for the elderly here. They account for about eighty percent of our business these days."

"Right," Russ said. "Of course." He noticed, not without a fair amount of anxiety, that Wayne had poured seven cups of water into the reservoir but only put two spoonfuls of coffee grounds into the filter. Without some divine intervention, in about five minutes he'd be tasked with forcing down a warm cup of dirt water.

Wayne pushed the start button and turned to face Russ. There was a different look in his eyes now, one of sudden resoluteness. Whatever small amount of light banter they had shared up to this point was now over. "We should get out to the desk," Wayne said. "We'll come back for the coffee later." Russ observed as Wayne brushed his hand across the upper buttons of his white shirt. Slowly, as if seeing it happen through some kind of drugged bleariness, Russ saw a number of stray coffee flecks tumble down into one of his double-breasted pockets.

Wayne led Russ over to a long counter with several stations behind it. They accessed the back area through a low flapping set of doors that resembled a mini saloon entrance. As Russ looked down the narrow aisle, he noticed that each station had its own unique look and feel. Some of the teller cubicles were outfitted with a set of twisted copper bars that must have dated back far into the previous century, while some included the more modern sheets of bulletproof glass.

"That crack right there," Wayne said, pointing to a quarter-sized dent in the glass, "was from one Albert Kleinman." He tapped the spot once with his finger then scurried on down the line.

"Was it, um, it was a... bullet?" Russ put a hand over his chest and pressed as though one had just entered there. His heart drummed in his ears.

"Ha! Lord no," Wayne said. "I don't think we've ever had a firearm used in here, knock on wood. That was nothing more than a surly temper and a stray boot heel."

"Was he missing money or something?" Russ asked.

"Nope," Wayne said. "He was an old-timer. The story goes he took one look at the new glass, took off his boot and banged it on the window out of disgust. Thought nobody could hear him or something. He was outraged about how darn fast things were changing around him. That was the last straw, I guess. This was two days after they made the transition. Progress has its detractors," he said. "That's why we kept some booths looking the old fashioned way."

"Were you here at that time?" Russ asked.

"Oh, God no! Are you kidding? That must have been like 1993 or something… I was barely even born." Wayne bent down and scooped some cracker crumbs off a table and into his palm. He discarded them in the waste can beneath the desk. "People around here like to chatter. Things get around, but you probably know that already."

Russ felt feverish all of a sudden. His heart raced. It was the idea of assault. Just the mention of a gun, even the slightest intimation of violence could get him worked up now. He couldn't even stand to watch the news. The memory of the shooting from two nights ago was still lurking just below his conscious mind. Judging from the tight knot in his abdomen, it was living right beneath his left rib cage.

"Are you alright?" Wayne asked.

"Yeah, I'm just tired I think."

"Well, we'll get you that coffee real soon," Wayne said. He pulled a rolling chair out from beneath a stooped desk, and after sweeping his hand up and down the backrest a few times, invited Russ to sit down. "This will be your, well, really *our* workspace for the next two weeks while we train."

The desk in front of Russ was filled with an odd assortment of paraphernalia. To the right of the computer was an electric mug warmer covered in a film of rusty orange and yellow stains, but there was no mug in sight. Briefly, but with great concern, Russ searched the desk for its counterpart without any luck. For a second he worried he'd never be able to stop searching for it, but then Wayne spoke up.

"You have everything you need right here," he said. Russ waited for a followup explanation but none came.

Two cubicles down a woman casually clicked away on her keyboard. The sound, being the only one currently available, took Russ's attention. Wayne noticed his wandering eye.

"That's Natalie," Wayne said. "Do you want to meet Natalie?"

"Um, sure," Russ said.

"Hi Natalie," Wayne called. After a few more keystrokes, Natalie looked up and wheeled her chair back so that she was more in their line of sight.

"Hello," Natalie said.

Natalie was wearing the type of sensible outfit Russ expected out of a place like RCB. She wore a green tweed skirt with a white blouse and a red cardigan on top. It was apparently Christmas year round at the Riegler Community Bank.

"Hi," she said again, this time inching closer in her chair. Now Russ could see that she was youngish, about Wayne's age probably maybe older, with long brown hair parted down the middle and slim, bare legs poking out of the skirt. "I'm Natalie," she said. "It's nice to meet you." She had a nice, warm smile and her general frame was plain but not at all unattractive. Ever since Molly left his ability to estimate beauty had been all out of whack. Sometimes he'd find himself fantasizing about a woman at the grocery store and then realize she was way too short or her teeth were crooked or she had a mustache. Desperation was a strange kaleidoscope. He was probably staring a bit too hard at Natalie because she shrugged one side of her sweater up higher on her shoulder, the way women sometimes do when they are worried about grazing eyes, and Russ felt an immediate wave of shame. "What's your name?" she asked.

"Huh? Oh, I'm Russ," he said.

"Hi Russ," she said, again with the warm smile. She waved, and Russ tried to see if she was wearing a wedding ring. She was too far away to tell.

"Hi Natalie," Russ said, trying to pull himself together. "I look forward to getting to know you, or, I mean working with you."

"Yeah," Natalie said. "Sure. Me too," and as she swiveled to the side Russ thought he noticed her give a little wink. "Well," she said, wheeling her way back in front of her desk, "I'll be right over here clicking away if you need anything. If you have any questions or whatever…" She trailed off as she disappeared back behind the cubicle walls. That wink. It was giving Russ hope somehow. He wasn't the only one who knew how dull this job was. It was the wink of an accomplice, a sidekick, a coffee drinker.

"Yeah," Russ said. "Sure thing. Thanks."

"Okay," Wayne said, moving right along. "This is your homebase." He was leaning forward, bearing down upon what looked like a giant anvil with a computer screen. Somebody had made the puzzling decision to keep the old metal cash register in place and attach a computer somehow. It looked as if someone had taken one of those radio consoles from the 1950s and welded a flat-screen TV on top. All things considered, after the other stuff he'd witnessed so far, this suddenly made perfect sense to him.

"It looks so heavy," Russ said.

"Well, you wouldn't want anyone to move it, would you?"

"I suppose not."

"Here is the on switch," Wayne said. He pressed a button on the side and the screen sparked to life, blooming from black to blue. "Step one!" he said, very pleased with himself. "It takes a few minutes." And as soon as he said it, Russ could tell he had no idea how to fill the time. As Wayne whistled softly and bobbed his head to an imaginary rhythm, Russ took the opportunity to inspect the other objects on the table. Spread out beneath the enormous computer, was one of those large paper calendars on which industrious people write important meetings or significant dates. Not only was it blank, but it was also two years old and covered in watery tea stains. January of 2017, Russ thought… that was when he first met Molly. Before he could sink too deeply into that malaise, gratefully, his attention veered back to the missing mug. Where was the little bastard?

The front door swung open and a tall man with a long beard and a wool newsboy cap strolled toward the counter.

"Crap," Wayne said. "I was wrong."

Russ felt a twinge of panic at being confronted with his first real customer. It was live now. There was no turning back. "What?" Russ said.

"That's not Harold Weber."

"Oh," Russ said. "Who is it?"

"Hello!" Wayne called. He stood up straighter and craned forward over the rail. His smile, his hips and shoulders all bristled with some jittery, electric animation. "I don't know who that is," he said, straining to identify him across the room. "Good morning, sir!"

"Hi," Russ said, reflexively, but the man was not interested in them. He was heading straight for Natalie.

Wayne seemed disturbed by the man's disregard, agitated that anybody would turn down his stellar service in favor of a lackluster option like Natalie. Not surprisingly, Wayne was one of those eager employees whose earnestness always made Russ feel a little sad. There was something pitiful in trying so hard to please a customer who would forget you the second they walked out the door.

"Well, look who it is," Natalie's disembodied voice said from behind her cubicle glass.

"Wow, Natalie," the man said. "My goodness. It's nice to see you."

"Haha!" Natalie said, "yeah. You don't have to say it like that. How are you?"

"Boy," the man said, "you look different, but your breath smells just the same!"

"Oh," Natalie said, "geez, that's an awfully sweet thing to say to somebody you haven't seen in a long time."

"So," Wayne broke in, "I should probably go over how Harold will want his bills. Harold will be in, rest assured." Russ was annoyed that Wayne had interrupted his listening to Natalie's conversation. He could not imagine where the dialogue would go from here, but he very much wanted to know.

Despite Wayne's insistence on filling time, the screen was now fully awake and blinking. It was ready for the password. "I think we can start now," Russ said. He had zero interest in hearing about Harold's bill preferences.

"The way you open the door without a transaction is you flip this lever underneath here." Wayne reached under the table and pulled on something there. The drawer flew open with a loud clang.

"Aaaa!" Russ said, and before he knew what he was doing, he had his hands over his ears. The ringing was back, the same low and extended chirp he heard after the gunshot. It felt like something that might result from a punch in the head, but Russ had never been in a fight before. Maybe he'd feel like this, like he was on guard from sort of awful brawl for the rest of his life.

"Russ?" Wayne said. "Russ?" he repeated, this time quieter. He tilted his head down and tried to look Russ in the eyes.

"I'm sorry," Russ said. He removed his hands. "I wasn't ready for that. That's really loud, isn't it? I mean, I'm sure that's louder than most people expect. It's very loud, don't you think?"

"I've never really thought of it before," Wayne said. "Are you alright?" He scanned the room, hoping to spot someone equipped to handle a panic attack but was disappointed to find that he was in charge, the first and last line of defense against any sort of human resource fiasco.

"Yeah, I… um, I'm sorry. I was just caught off guard, that's all. I was thinking we'd just learn about how to start up the computer and get into some of the programs or something…"

"There will be plenty of time for that," Wayne said, happy to find himself back in a line of thought he could navigate.

Natalie's discussion with the man started back up again. "As I said, I wasn't thinking about your heart in those terms," the man said. Russ wished he could see Natalie's expression. Something didn't seem right about the interaction. Nothing was adding up. It was strange that he already felt protective of Natalie, but he did somehow.

"Okay," Wayne said, drowning out their conversation again. "Before you reach into the drawer for the cash, you have to put a little moisture on your fingers." He dabbed two fingers into a small dish with a yellow sponge inside. Russ had been wondering after the purpose of the dish. That was at least one question answered. "This allows you to separate the bills. They're so crisp when they're new, and they always stick together."

For the next few minutes, Russ was forced to watch as Wayne peeled bill after bill from the drawer and stacked it on the cluttered table. "That's 1500 dollars," Wayne said. "Ten hundreds. Five fifties, ten twenties and five tens."

Russ was losing focus. He kept drifting in and out of consciousness. The murder kept flashing into his head. He wanted to hear Natalie's conversation. The sound of the gun, isolated from all other noises, kept creeping back to him. Maybe he should see someone. He'd told the police everything he saw and knew, but they didn't seem satisfied. He hoped they wouldn't come back. What exactly were the clinical signs of PTSD?

"All right, so now we'll do Doris Forney," Wayne said. "She likes all small bills." He pinched Mr. Weber's bills in half the long way and stuffed them back into the drawer. "She'll get her standard 950. She'll swear it's 1000, but as I mentioned, she's not all with it."

"Right," Russ said. The new matter that was now taking up all of his concentration was the green Post-It note on the corner of Wayne's computer screen. "Dad's appointment Thursday at 4 pm," it read. It somehow humanized Wayne, made Russ want to inquire about it further. Everyone has a dad. This could be a way to relate to Wayne. Russ needed something like that, an anchor, if he was to weather any more of this inane training.

"Did you get that?" Wayne was saying. "Fourteen fives. I know that's crazy, but we're talking about Doris Forney here. You'll get plenty more like her." He put all of the money back in the drawer and closed it again. This time he made extra sure not to let it bang shut. Russ appreciated this tiny gesture of sympathy. "Now," he said, "from the top. You try it now. Are you ready?"

"I guess so," Russ said, unable to stifle a yawn.

"Start by opening the drawer. You remember how. Then just think... Harold. Weber. Picture Harold Weber. I'll give you a hint. Start with the big bills first."

Russ flipped the switch under the counter and caught the drawer as it came swinging out at him. He dipped his fingers into the drawer and began skimming the money out.

"Wait!" Wayne hollored. "The moisture! Don't forget the sponge! Let's start over."

All at once Russ had a splitting headache. He couldn't picture Harold Weber. He'd never met Harold Weber. There was no way he was getting that coffee today. He just knew it. Try not to even think about it, he told himself. It will only drive you mad. They didn't need another Doris Forney on their hands.

3

Russ hadn't been able to go out the back door to the alleyway since the murder happened. This meant that he was lugging his garbage down the front steps, through the carpeted and deodorized hallways, then hauling it all the way around the gate in back and out to the dumpsters. It was crazy, Russ knew, but he just wasn't ready to face the rickety stairwell that led to the eerie alley where all that blood had been. It was like the precarious pathway was becoming a mirror for his own spooked and twisted insides. He hadn't been eating well or having the right bowel movements in a week.

When he tossed the trash into the dumpster a rat, plump and long as a loaf of bread, came darting out at him from the darkness beneath. Russ stumbled back, feeling the coarse grey hair scrape his ankle as it bolted for the fence on the other side. The way it leapt and crammed its furry body through the small diamond shape in the chain links didn't look natural. The rat's behavior was not the only thing out of whack. He was also aware that the frantic pace he was using to reach the front sidewalk must have appeared suspicious as well. A shudder raced through him as he slowed to a less erratic stride.

Thank God the front of his apartment did not possess the same dark and chilling effect. The sun was just high and bright enough to take the edge off the crisp wind blowing from the north. Russ had no idea where he was headed. It didn't matter. The point was to get some exercise and clear his head, and if that was the idea Russ felt lucky that his quest would play out under such an azure and sympathetic sky. Russ rolled the sleeves up on the Wellton College sweatshirt he wore. It was the type of drowsy Sunday morning when a sedate wanderer might notice that even certain objects can be said to lie sleeping. Jacob Wexler's lawnmower hadn't moved from its resting spot beside the shed since early September. Frank Osborne's leaning stack of bricks still slumbered beside the base of a crumbling chimney waiting for a dormant worker to be roused into action. The lingering outline of a long-presiding ladder burned into Charles Schaffer's rooftop stands as a reminder of man's best-laid intentions. People were always starting and abandoning projects in Wellton. Russ didn't know if that was because Wellton had a way of breeding that type of inertia into people or if that type of inertia attracted people who were already searching for a town like Wellton to bury their ambitions.

He'd told Officer Lang everything he knew about the night Kirby Baxter was killed. The Baxters, being one of only a few families of color in the entire county, and being a recent addition to the Valley View trailer park, had been on Wesley Lang's radar from day one. During their conversation, Russ noted that Wesley's pants fit him the way a toddler's or a very old man's sometimes do. His skinny legs knocked around loosely inside the fabric, appearing as if all the muscle and flesh had either withered away or not grown in yet. Russ felt sorry for him. It could not have been easy getting folks to take you seriously with such a delicate frame like that.

The Baxters, Wesley Lang told Russ, had come down from Atlantic City, and Russ should know what that meant. Wesley raised his eyebrows. He did know, didn't he? Russ wanted to say, "someone can finally teach me how to play poker?" but he stopped himself. Wesley said that folks don't leave beach towns like Atlantic City to come to Wellton for its weather or their famous homemade pretzels. Russ couldn't think of anyone who had ever come for those reasons, but again he kept his mouth shut. Wesley spoke like a man who had trouble activating his imagination. In his mind everyone already shared his opinions, and so everything he said came out as insult or assumption. It wasn't on purpose. That was the size of his universe. Still, Russ told him as much as he could, as politely as he could, about everything. Whatever it took to make the situation to go away as quickly as possible.

"And you said he was African American, the shooter?" Lang asked. He'd been scribbling something down on his notepad for a long time. It seemed he was writing down three times as many words as Russ spoke.

"I didn't," Russ said.

"You didn't?" Wesley asked. "You said that he was wearing African… I mean, black?"

"No, nothing African or black."

"I could have sworn…" Wesley said. He stopped writing for the first time in about five minutes, then started right back up again. "But the victim was black?"

"Yes," Russ said.

"Right, and how far did you say you were from the perpetrator?"

"I don't know," Russ said, "he was already running away when I looked out the window."

"So, he was pretty far away," Wesley said.

"I guess you could say that."

"And you only saw him from behind?"

"That's true," Russ said.

"Right. Okay." Wesley was still writing. He flipped page after page on his tiny notepad and kept right on going. The constant repetition was almost mesmerizing.

"What are you writing?" Russ asked.

"Notes," Wesley said. "So, you can't be certain of his appearance or um… his description?"

"I wouldn't say that," Russ said. "There are lights in the alley."

"Lights?"

"Well, yes. A streetlight. One of them."

"Okay, and so when the suspect was under those lights…" He paused and looked up at Russ. Both of them were trying to figure out what the other was thinking.

"When he was under the light I could see that he was kind of big and a little awkward. He had so many layers of clothing on."

"Awkward," Wesley said.

"Yeah, I mean he seemed out of place. I don't know, like he was unsure or unfit to be where he was or to be doing what he was doing."

"That's a judgment call," Wesley said.

"Sure," Russ said, "okay," and he meant to say, "but not the color of his skin. Skin color is not an abstract thing," but he couldn't do it. He couldn't look at Lang. He was trying but his nerves wouldn't let him. It was more than just a mental hurdle. The strain was physical. Every time he tried, his neck dipped grudgingly to the side or his pupil started to twitch. He wanted to disagree, but disagreeing with a cop was not a good strategy for making the symptoms of an anxiety attack go away.

"You said he had a lot of clothing on and that he was…" he glanced down at his pad again. "... running away, and you only saw him from the window…"

"I saw his hand," Russ said, "the one holding the gun. He had a lot of layers on, but he wasn't wearing any gloves. I got a good look at his hands."

Wesley sighed. He put the pad back in the front pocket of his shirt and hiked his baggy pants up higher on his slender waist. His hands were so long and feminine, like prickly sewing needles. "Well," he said, "if you have any more premonitions or recollections about the killer's profile…"

"I won't," Russ said. He wanted so badly to make sure he didn't have to talk about this again.

"You are the only eye witness," Wesley said. "Give it some time."

"I don't want any more time," Russ said. He looked at Wesley with as much desperation as he could, imploring him to stay away. "Please," he said. But then right away he realized that either he had sent the wrong message or he'd sent the right one but Lang didn't know how to recognize it.

"I know it's hard," Wesley said, and the fact that he seemed to have genuine concern in his eyes made everything even worse. "But we're here for you, and we won't give up on you."

After that Russ just sort of felt himself go limp and cold. When Wesley offered him his card and told him to stay in touch, Russ just nodded and took the card. As soon as he climbed his stairs and got back inside his apartment he wadded it up and threw it in the trash can. The trash was filling up. He'd have to take it out again soon. And then the cycle of anxiety and distress would start all over again.

The charred remains of the Holcomb house were up ahead on the left. Russ could see the blackened outline of the two-story house, the scorched and hollow windows and the singed lawn in front. Death had visited the neighborhood more than once in the month of October. About five days before Kirby's life was taken, three members of the Holcomb household had gotten trapped inside as an aggressive fire engulfed their colonial home and burned it half to the ground. The whole neighborhood came out to witness it go up in flames. Small children next door especially loved the fire hoses and all the blaring sirens. One little girl lost a shoe, and for the next few days the search for the sneaker became as big of an event as comforting the mourners and laying to rest the dead. They did finally locate it. It was found on top of one of the garage roofs where she had climbed in order to search for a kitten someone had said might have survived the blaze. It made the evening news and everything.

As Russ got closer he noticed that a young couple was huddled outside the remains on the sidewalk. There would have been nothing out of the ordinary about the scene except the man and woman were clinging so tightly to one another and both of them appeared to be of Hispanic origin. Through the fur-lined hood the woman wore, Russ could see her light brown cheeks and neck. One did not often come across people of such origins on Slate Street. Both were dressed in heavy winter coats too warm for the mild weather. They had their arms entwined so high above their shoulders that it looked more as if they were hugging each other's heads instead of torsos. It was partially this irregular tableau and partly because the smiles they gave him were so affectionate that Russ slow down. They seemed to be intrigued with his sweatshirt, particularly the man who nudged the woman with his elbow and nodded toward the writing in the center of it.

"Good morning," Russ said. He stopped a few feet away and moved next to them on the grass.

"Hello," the woman said. "I'm Flores. Sorry, I mean Teresa." The two of them untangled and the man brought his arm around to greet him.

"I'm Daniel Flores," he said. He looked to be about twenty-five or six. His brown eyes and his sturdy posture were very handsome, but when Russ went to shake his hand he noticed how rough his fingers were. One of his knuckles had some dried blood on it and his thumbnail was purple.

"I'm Russ," Russ said. "Cooper. I live about three blocks down the street."

"It's a very nice street," Daniel said. He turned and looked at the fallen home behind them. Somebody had poked a square metal frame into the grass that looked exactly like a For Sale sign, but there was nothing printed on it. It was just a set of white squares with nothing on them.

"It's not too bad," Russ said. Daniel was looking at the house like he longed for someone to turn back time, while Teresa looked at him in that tender but obscured way people sometimes do when they know for sure that a place, a person or a feeling is gone for good but don't know how to break the news.

"It's quiet here," Teresa said. Her accent was thicker and sweeter than Daniel's. She put one hand on Daniel's shoulder and one on the blank For Sale sign beside her. "You're the first one we have seen out walking today." Though it was clear that they were not from around Wellton, their vocabulary and grammar were very impressive.

It wasn't that Russ assumed all people from Mexico were incapable of speaking proper English. He knew they were, but he had never seen it firsthand. To Russ's knowledge there were exactly four Mexican people who lived in Wellton. All of them worked at the one Mexican restaurant in town, and all of them, despite clearly being the most knowledgeable and experienced in the realm of Mexican dining, were relegated to back-of-the-house duty as line-cooks, where they spoke Spanish exclusively and perspired incessantly while a white married couple managed the front floor, ran the books and cut all of the paychecks. This was the extent of Russ's awareness when it came to people of hispanic descent and their language tendencies.

"Everyone is at church," Russ said. "It's prime time."

Teresa smiled and nodded. She, like her husband, was also rather young and good looking. Her hazel eyes were kind and her figure was well-proportioned, but much like her husband's gnarled hands, the pocked skin around her forehead and the wrinkled flesh around her mouth betrayed her. It was odd, Russ thought, how smallness affected different people in different ways. Both Teresa and Daniel were rather short but in a plainly endearing way. Whereas Lang's smallness played as shameful, theirs came off as darling.

"We were looking at this home," Daniel said, as if this fundamentally excused him from missing church on a Sunday.

Russ put his hands in his pockets. "Did you know the Holcombs?" he asked in a cautious and tentative manner.

"No," Daniel said, "but we heard what happened. Mister Rolland told us. Do you know James Rolland?" Maybe his accent was rougher than Teresa's. When he got excited his words came faster and his pitch rose a few octaves.

"No," Russ said. "I've never heard of him."

"When we found this place we knew we had to have it," Daniel said. Teresa's arm began gliding up and down Daniel's back. She nodded in rhythm to her soothing touch.

"Our nephew's house burned down back in Mexico," Teresa said. She lowered her head and buried it in Daniel's wooly coat.

"My brother lost his life in the fire," Daniel said, "and my nephew had nowhere else to go so we took him in,"

"His mom died two years earlier in a horrible car crash," Teresa said.

"Wow," Russ said. "That's a lot to deal with. I'm so sorry. That sounds very sad, but he's lucky to have you."

"A few months ago Arturo, that's our nephew, got accepted to Dickinson College. You know Dickinson College, yes?"

"I have heard of it, yes," Russ said. "It's in Harrisburg?"

"Carlisle," Daniel said. "You heard of it? It's real, yeah?"

"Yes," Russ said again. "I've heard of it."

"Carlisle is not far from Harrisburg," Teresa said.

"Yes," Russ said, "that's right."

"Arturo was accepted into Dickinson a few months ago," Daniel said. "They gave him a full scholarship. All tuition paid. I have no idea why, but they were the only ones to do that for him. It was an enormous blessing. So we followed him here."

"Here we are," said Teresa. "We left our rented apartment in Texas and came to help him get settled in. We plan on staying. We promised to take care of him. This is a new life for us, too."

Texas? No wonder their English was so strong. Russ hadn't even entertained the notion that they could be from anywhere other than Mexico. He'd have to ponder the roots of that error and work through it later.

"We tried finding affordable homes around Harrisburg or Carlisle," Daniel said, "but the only ones that were in our price range were in the barrio."

"The what?" Russ said.

Daniel snapped his fingers. "Sorry. The ghetto."

Russ nodded. "Oh, yeah!" he said, "Right. I've heard that."

"Someone told us that Harrisburg, they had the highest suicide rate in the country," Daniel said.

"That used to be true. I think it went down," Russ said. "I remember seeing a lot of places from Arizona on the list last time it was published."

Daniel tilted his head and frowned. He looked sideways at Russ, unsure why he would have such data at his fingertips. "I like psychology," Russ said. "It doesn't usually come in handy, but sometimes."

"We started widening our search," Teresa said, "and we ended up here. It was a complete coincidence. Totally random, not like Mr. Rolland said about the train station."

"What do you mean? Train station?" Russ said.

"Mr. Rolland asked us if we saw an advertisement for job openings in a Mexican train station. He thought maybe someone from Wellton had secretly passed around flyers looking for cheap labor in Mexico."

Russ lowered his head. He let it dangle there as he shook it back and forth.

"I said, 'Mr. Rolland, with all due respect, there is no train from Mexico to Wellton.' We're not even actually from Mexico. We're from El Paso.' I told him but he didn't believe us."

"He didn't believe you were from El Paso?" Russ asked.

"I'm not sure," Daniel said. "I think he didn't believe us that El Paso was in Texas. He was pretty sure it was in Mexico."

Russ raised his head. He laughed, but when he noticed that Teresa and Daniel were not joining in he stopped. "I'm sorry," Russ said. "It's just. I don't know what to say." Russ put his head down again and sighed.

"I'm a carpenter," Daniel said. "We found an ad in the newspaper for what we think is this place, but we couldn't find a listing price. I know it can't be that much. Maybe 50,000 in this state? What do you think?"

"Tops," Russ said. "You could probably go lower."

He pointed over his shoulder. "I can fix this place up. I was betting that if I offered them 30,000 dollars they would take it and leave happy. They wouldn't have to clear the property or anything. I can fix it up myself."

"That sounds like a solid plan," Russ said. "Good idea. Did it work?"

"We called the number on the listing," Teresa said, "and the next day, yesterday, two men came out to show us around."

"Mr. Rolland?" Russ asked.

"Yes," Teresa said "James was his first name."

"And who else?"

"A police officer," Teresa said.

"Do you remember his name?" asked Russ.

Teresa looked at Daniel. "Was it Walter something?"

"Wesley," Daniel said.

"Wesley Lang?" Russ said.

"You know him?" Daniel said.

"Yes," Russ said. "I know him."

"Maybe you could talk to him," Daniel said.

"Well," Russ said, "I'd rather not. I've already talked to him too much this week."

Daniel and Teresa exchanged an uneasy look with one another.

"It's just that he didn't seem to understand our offer," Teresa said.

"No, I'm sure he didn't," Russ said.

"He suggested that we look somewhere else for property," Daniel said. "Someplace called Valley View. Do you know where that is?"

"Yes," Russ said. "It's a trailer park."

"Trailer park?" Teresa said. "I've heard of those, but I don't think I've actually seen one before."

"Funny," Russ said. "It's basically the same idea here."

"What do you mean? What is it like, exactly?" asked Teresa.

Russ took a deep breath. He looked at Daniel. "A barrio."

"We thought so," Daniel said.

Russ couldn't look them in the eyes, and so he looked back at the house. The white siding around the front door looked like a giant cake with a hole punched in the middle. Someone had scooped out a section and eaten the frosting. It would be hard to fix the place up without starting all over again. It was when he looked back in their direction that he saw a woman coming toward them across the street. She was not wearing any jacket at all, which made her sort of shrink in against her own body for warmth. The gesture also made her look tiny and a little frightened. She was carrying a bright green bible in one hand which stood out against her gray dress and cream-colored shirt. Russ had never seen a bible that color before. It made it look fake, like a child's toy.

"James was the one who told us he was holding off on selling the property right now," Teresa said. She and Daniel couldn't see the woman coming because they were facing the opposite direction.

"Oh yeah?" Russ said. "And who is this James Rolland exactly?"

"The county building code inspector," Daniel said.

"I see," said Russ. "And why did he say they were holding off?" The woman was definitely coming straight for them. She put the bible up to her breast and hugged it there. She was treating it as if someone had threatened to rip it from her hands.

"Something about a 'mortality violation,'" Daniel said.

"Mortality?" Russ asked.

"Yeah, have you ever heard of that?" Daniel asked.

"No, never," Russ said.

"He said that if somebody dies in a house they have to wait at least two months before they can sell the property," Teresa said.

"That seems strange," Russ said.

"Do you know things about the building codes or the inspecting that goes on here?" Teresa asked.

"No," Russ said, "not really,"

"Could you find out?" Daniel asked. Again he turned his attention on the Wellton College stitching in the middle of his sweatshirt.

"I could try…" and then before Russ could finish his sentence the bible woman was upon them. She marched right in behind Dan and Teresa, snapping both feet together as she came to a halt. There was an almost military precision to it.

"Good afternoon," the woman said. She had a chipper, sing-song type of tone. "It's a lovely day for a walk after church, isn't it?" she said. When nobody gave much of a response, save Teresa who smiled and gave a courteous "si," the woman started over again. "I'm sorry," she said. "I should introduce myself. I'm Jennifer Healy." They each nodded in return but offered little more in the way of a reciprocal greeting. "Did you all come from church, too? Where do you all attend?" After some time had passed in silence she stepped back a pace and tried a third time. She was determined to get a conversation going. "I walked all the way to St. Benedict and back this morning. I'm on my way back now. I only live about three more blocks west over on Willow Street."

"That must be more than three miles," Russ said.

"That's right!" Jennifer said. "Three-point-three to be exact! You must be from around here." She turned to face Russ directly, boxing out Dan and Teresa from her little monologue. She was so small and timid looking in her bleak little church outfit. Her shoulders were like those of a bird, which is to say it was as if she didn't have any at all. Her gaunt profile gave the impression that one could wrap their arms around her body twice. It was astounding that a person this frail had walked so far.

"We were looking at the house," Daniel said. It was a drab and dry tone, the type used to signal that a person wants to be left alone, but Jennifer did not take the hint.

"I can see that," Jennifer said. She turned and looked at the house and for the first time it dawned on her that she may have wandered into a solemn scene. "Oh," she said. "I see." She pivoted from Russ to face Dan and Teresa who had both turned their backs on her. "Did you know the Holcomb family, may I ask?"

Dan and Teresa shook their heads. "We want to buy the house," Daniel said, still facing away from Jennifer.

"See," Jennifer said. "I knew it. I knew I was doing the right thing stopping here to chat." She looked at each of them in turn, then spun and gave them all the same bug-eyed smile again. She seemed to be shocked that people weren't responding the way she imagined. "My pastor would be so proud," she continued. "See, his sermon today, it was on being a good neighbor. It's all right here of course." She opened her neon green bible and began flipping through it furiously. "Here it is!" she exclaimed. "Hebrews chapter thirteen, verses one and two. 'Keep on loving one another as brothers and sisters. Do not forget to show hospitality to strangers, for by so doing some people have shown hospitality to angels without knowing it.' You see? Isn't that beautiful?"

It was. Russ had to admit it. As far as bible sentiments go, that was a very nice one. Even Dan and Teresa turned around and smiled.

"That is nice," Teresa said.

"I like that," Russ said. Daniel nodded.

Jennifer was elated by this turnaround. She snapped the book shut. "Should we all pray together over this house?" Russ looked at Daniel who looked at Teresa who looked back at Russ. It was clear that Russ should be the one to say no.

"Um," Russ said. "Maybe not right now. We were sort of in the middle of something so no thank you."

Teresa and Dan seemed pleased with this answer. Teresa moved closer to Dan and Dan put his arm around her.

"Okay. That's okay," Jennifer said. "At least I asked." But she was not good at hiding her displeasure. Her mouth puckered up and her eyes squeezed shut. "It's just that. It's just... well, do you know what Pastor Hughes said today?"

Everyone shook their heads. It was getting cold just standing still there, and Russ put his hands inside the sleeves of his sweater to keep warm.

"He told a story. Maybe you guys have heard about it," Jennifer said. "In Phoenix Arizona they are trying out these new self-driving delivery trucks." She paused to see if any of them were showing any signs of recognition. When nobody responded she kept going. "They have these trucks that run on GPS and motion sensors all by themselves, no drivers needed. It's supposed to make the delivery process more efficient and precise. I guess they were doing a trial run in Phoenix, and do you know what happened?"

"No," Daniel said. "What happened?"

"I'll tell you," Jennifer said. "People attacked them. They threw rocks and bricks. Some people even popped their tires. Two separate men came out of their homes with shotguns and threatened to shoot the things up. Just right there, in broad daylight! Can you imagine?"

Russ shrugged. "Well, I mean -"

"Is that any way to treat a neighbor!" Jennifer interrupted. "With bricks and a shotgun? Has the world gone mad? What is wrong with us?"

"In your story, your pastor's story, the robotic trucks are the neighbors?" Russ said.

"I assume so, yes," Jennifer said.

"Okay, well what about the former drivers who used to actually drive the trucks and perform all the duties and get paid money to feed their families? Aren't they neighbors too?"

"Well, yes," Jennifer said, "but - "

"It would be a different story if the billionaires behind this business venture replaced the humans with the trucks and then compensated those workers for their loss or created new positions to keep them earning a paycheck while their robots took over, but that isn't the case." Russ could feel his heart start pumping and his thoughts begin galloping faster just as they always did during debates in his philosophy classes at Wellton College. "Those human workers, those neighbors, have nowhere else to go for a means of survival. People are already very depressed in Arizona."

"Oh, all right," Jennifer said, her voice rising in tandem with her narrow eyebrows. "so it's okay to break something or destroy something when things don't go your way? What is this world coming to?"

"I'd be more afraid, Jennifer," Russ said, "if people stopped acting out in these situations. The world has gone crazy when people cease to fight against tyranny and oppression. That's when you should be afraid. That's when we're really doomed!"

Jennifer's expression went blank and pale. A distant gaze came into her eyes, and she closed them so she wouldn't have to keep facing them all like this. When she opened them again she looked wounded but resolved, like a boxer who has taken some punches but is still determined to continue the next round. There was no doubt that Jennifer Healy was a caring person. It was just that, Russ thought, she placed the caring upon people and things that were less deserving than others. For example, he could picture her complaining to an attendant about a subpar meal as their plane went down. It was almost sweet…

"I'm sorry," Russ said. "I didn't mean to get that heated. I apologize." Russ apologized to Dan and Teresa too, who seemed more shocked than concerned or upset. Dan ran his hand over his face in a slow, tired circle. He pulled at the corner of his eyes and took a deep breath.

Jennifer straightened her shirt. She brushed her hands down her dress and placed the bible down at her waist. "You certainly have a very bizarre way of looking at the world," she said.

"I could say the same about you," Russ said. "And yet we live only three blocks away from one another."

Jennifer's mouth popped open, flapping there for a moment before she snapped it shut again. She'd been offended by the statement, but couldn't place exactly why. "Well, okay then," she said. "You all have a nice day." She had to walk around and behind all of them to keep heading down the sidewalk. For a few seconds there was a clumsy obstacle course of bodies and limbs happening as she zigzagged her way by.

"You too," said Teresa.

"It was nice meeting you," Dan said.

Almost the second Jennifer was out of earshot, Dan started up right where they had left off. "So, do you know anybody who could help us figure out these county building codes? We'd really like to buy this property faster than two months."

Russ had to chuckle. He couldn't help it. This time Teresa laughed too.

"You still want to live here?" Russ asked. "Are you sure?"

"There are worse things than church ladies," Dan said.

"I could make a compelling argument on the other side, but I doubt you're in the mood to hear it right now," Russ said, and they all had a good laugh together.

"Psychology?" Dan asked.

"Something like that," Russ said.

Russ liked them a lot. He felt better now. In the end, somehow, the walk had done exactly what it was supposed to do. Maybe it was divine intervention.

"It's a burned down house that needs my help," Dan said. "I'm a carpenter. This is what I do. I'm not a doctor or a fireman, though sometimes I wish I was. I know it sounds funny, but I feel like if I save this home, it will be like saving a little piece of my brother, Raul. He would have understood."

"Also," Teresa added. "It was a bitch getting Arturo here to America. I'm just being honest. I'm not turning back now."

"I get it," Russ said. "I want this to happen for you guys. I'm no expert, but I'll see what I can do."

"You have a college degree," Daniel said.

"No, not really," Russ said.

"Really?" Teresa said. "I thought you did for sure."

"That's a very kind assumption, but I'm not worthy of it."

"You have a high school degree though, right?" Dan said.

"That I did manage," Russ said. "I have one of those." And then it became apparent why he had been so interested in his sweatshirt.

"Teresa and I never graduated. We don't have any idea how to figure this out. You must know more than we do."

"I will try, but I can't let you put it like that. I might know more about books or research, but you get to work with your own two hands for a living. At least you get to see the fruits of your labors right in front of you, piece by piece. There's no mystery where your sweat is going. No robots can take your place…" Russ paused in thought. He looked down at his own hands, wondering how long it would take for his hands to look the way Daniel's did lifting nothing but someone else's money at the bank. "Yeah, and there isn't a chance in hell I could fix this house up. You know what I mean?"

"Don't say hell," Daniel said.

"I mean, I can't even clean a window," Russ said. "Wait, why can't I say hell?"

"That lady," Daniel said. "Jennifer might come back."

"Hahaha!" Russ laughed. "Teresa's the one who said 'bitch'"

"She's Teresa, though," Daniel said. "Look at her. The devil would never come for a woman like her."

Russ blushed. It was so unusual to find a couple so in love. They didn't exist outside fairy tales, Russ thought, or maybe it was only that they didn't appear north of El Paso. "Fair enough. I'll keep things very wholesome," he said.

Dan gave Russ his phone number and then they said their goodbyes. As Russ walked home he felt for the first time in a long while that his life had purpose. He smoked a cigarette and thought about helping Teresa and Daniel work on the property after they were cleared to purchase. Maybe he could carry the boards over and hand them to Daniel. He'd seen that on construction sites before, a little guy balancing a long plank twice his size across his shoulder as he tried to turn around without cracking someone's skull or breaking a car window. That was honest work, and it taught simple consideration.

That night Russ did the only thing he knew how to do to help the Flores family. He googled "County of Wellton Vacant Building Codes." He read every document he could find, scanning for any words like 'death' or 'fatality' or even 'mortality.' There was absolutely nothing. He scribbled some notes on a piece of paper and put it by his bed. In the morning he'd call the number Dan and Teresa gave him before he left and let them know that someone was lying.

4

The last person to be murdered in Wellton County was a thirty-year-old drug dealer with a black widow tattoo under one eye and a rap sheet dating all the way back to a string of armed burglaries in middle school. Jerrod Blummer was his name. He was killed in 2009 right when Valley View started making national news as one of the poorest communities on the east coast. That was the same year Russ and his oldest pal, Richie, first started skipping school to hang out in Richie's dingy basement, watching stoner movies like Half Baked and choking down bottles of mango-flavored Mad Dog 20/20. That was how they came to know Blummer. After school, between last period and bike rides to the grocery store to buy grape soda and Swedish Fish, a small pack of wayward boys would kill time at the gas station down the street from Wellton High. They'd smoke squares and maybe pretend to skateboard a little bit or strike up a crude game of Hacky Sack before somebody from the school or a manager at the mini-mart would come over and chase them off for loitering. In back of the gas station, tucked in beside an old T-shirt factory, was the A-Plus Liquor Store. The irony of the store's name, with its allusion educational success, was not lost on the motley crew of mostly D and F students. It was there, during the spring of junior year, that Jerrod Blummer would be waiting outside the door almost every day. He was a feeble and seedy looking guy with long dirty hair and an Iron Maiden tank top that used to be white but had turned brown and yellow from all the constant wearing. He had the kind of shriveled body and sallow desperation that let a boy know he was telling the truth when he offered to buy you alcohol and keep it quiet for a five percent hike in the cost. So for a few months, from about March until May of 2009, Blummer was the guy all of the punks and ruffians like Russ and Richie went to for their Mad Dog or Mickeys or St. Ides Special Brews.

It was unclear how much money Jerrod made that spring, skimming an extra dollar or two from every hood who needed a fix, but between that and his drug dealing, it still wasn't enough to spare his life. Sometime right before school ended that year, Jerrod Blummer was found shot to death outside on his best friend's deck in Valley View. The story came out that Jerrod had arrived home drunk late one night and raided his roommate's refrigerator. When his roommate, a man so inconsequential that his name was immediately lost to obscurity, came rambling into the kitchen high and hungry and noticed that his leftover tacos were missing, he reached for his revolver, chased Blummer out into the warm evening and pulled the trigger. It seemed so twisted that after all of his robberies and carjackings and drug dealings, that he would be laid to rest for eating some wilted fajitas. Russ couldn't help but think it made a cruel bit of sense. The universe was sarcastic like that sometimes. The sad thing was that Russ and Richie had really come to like Jerrod. There was something about the way he looked out for them, how he always made sure that nobody was watching when he came out with their drinks and how he took the time to always wrap the bottles nicely and hand them off with such a spirit of caring. His death made them feel a real sense of loss and sorrow. "Be safe out there," he would always say before slinking off again into the shadows. But outside of Russ and Richie there was really nobody around who felt a single thing for Jerrod Blummer, which was why Wesley Lang wasn't concerned about the matter and why there was very little attention or coverage of the incident. There was no heat coming off Jerrod Blummer. It had all seemed so inevitable anyway. Here was a lifelong criminal who had already been written off as worn out and broken and useless from a very young age. Kirby Baxter; however, was a different story altogether. He was a sweet kid with good grades and parents who loved him enough to fight for justice. There would be hell to pay for this one if the killer was never found and Lang knew it.

When Russ pulled up outside Richie's mom's house on Lindale Street it was after nine. Evening had a way of making the place look even more foreboding than it did in the daytime. The house was big but old and run-down with peeling green paint and caving walls that made it appear as if it was slowly sinking into its own muddy grave. He'd lived there his entire life and sometimes it seemed as if he might just die there if the place held up long enough. His dad had been gone from the picture for a long time, and his mom kept the two of them barely afloat through a combination of part-time work as a mail sorter at the post office and disability checks from the state for her muscular dystrophy. Richie would have moved out by now if he hadn't been his mom's caretaker and only confidant. The constant strain and dysphoria of his duties were what led him to start drinking heavily at fifteen. It was around this time that Russ and Richie started spending a lot of time together. Richie Hess and Russ Cooper. Back then some of their classmates started calling them "R and R." It was a good joke because it was ridiculous and backward in just the right way. Everyone knew they were anything but restful and relaxing when they got going. Calling them R and R was silly in the same way it was silly to call a really fat man Tiny.

Russ honked his horn. He could hardly hear the sound of it over all the knocking and rattling going on under his hood. Whenever he was stopped or idling the engine coughed and rumbled so loudly that Russ was certain it was just going to perish right where it stood, but then it would wheeze back to life just in time to get rolling again. There was a metaphor there for his own fitful existence that Russ tried not to think about too hard but always failed. He was stuck in the dismal thought again when Richie came stumbling out his front door and lumbered for the car. For the most part he looked the same as he had in high school with the exception that he limped now on his right leg and his stomach had grown even more pregnant and distended with booze and frozen pizzas. Russ was with him the night that he hurt his leg. They were both hammered, and so It was almost comical the way Richie had stepped off the curb when he wasn't ready and gone hurtling into the street. It was funny because it looked like his belly was what did it, like the weight of his swollen gut had thrown him off balance and tossed him out into the road. It became less comical when it was clear that he was hurt worse than they first thought and he didn't have the healthcare to take care of it.

"Aaaaaye," Richie said as he opened the door and began the painful process of lowering himself into place. He grabbed hold of the roof of the car, nearly tipping it over as he slid one butt cheek onto the seat with a grunt. Next, he hoisted his good leg in and then dragged his bum one in behind it. By the time he heaved his body sideways and stretched for the door to yank it shut, he'd already spent a full minute getting settled. His squat and hefty body fit into the space between the door and console like a bowling ball into a baseball glove, scarcely enough room to burp.

"You good?" Russ said, waiting for Richie's breathing to stop sputtering and level out.

"Shit yes," Richie said. "What's taking you so long?"

"Oh, right," Russ said, adopting a bad French accent, "Oui, your precious time will not be wasted, monsieur. Where am I taking you this evening, monsieur? The Louvre? La Sorbonne?"

"Don't talk like that when you know we're fucking heading to Valley View," Richie said, "It's disrespectful."

"Really?" Russ said as he steered out onto Lindale and headed north. "How is that?"

"I don't know," Richie said, "it just seems like your taunting the land or the people or something. You're mocking them." He leaned back and shoved his hands inside his puffy jacket pockets. He was wearing the white Adidas jacket with the black stripes down the arms that he wore all the time. It must have been at least ten years old. Russ can remember telling him back in high school that thing was too stained and smelly to wear anymore. Its overall color had gone from snow white to sooty gray, but Richie refused to throw it out. He said it still served its purpose. *It still keeps me warm, doesn't it?*

"I didn't realize you had such a deep affection for the place."

Richie pulled a cigarette pack out from one of his pockets and cracked the window. "It just seems insensitive under the circumstances," he said. He lit a cigarette with his lighter and tossed it on top of the dashboard.

Richie's words, as they sometimes did, hit harder than Russ expected. He absorbed the condemnation like a blow to his chin. "Yeah," he said. "I guess you're right." He lowered his voice, leaning into his remorse. "Yeah," he whispered again, trailing off. "Fuck."

Richie could do that sometimes, catch you off guard with his random benevolence. It was one of the things that Russ liked most about him, his ability to always keep people guessing. He'd been like that for as long as Richie knew him, a chaotic hellraiser one minute and a mindful savant the next. Ever since Russ had told him about the murder, Richie had been extra thoughtful and circumspect.

They drove toward Route 422 in silence, smoking cigarettes and listening to the wind come rustling in through their windows. There weren't any streetlights on that stretch, just a few houses with lamps on in their living rooms or maybe a couple of mothy bulbs dangling outside vacant garage doors. It was a treacherous road with several tight curves and blind hilltops. Any manner of unseen deer or possums or groundhogs could be hiding just around the bend. You didn't have to look far to see the warning signs. The craggy banks on either side were littered with flattened roadkill floating in milky rivulets left behind from all the recent rain. A gloomy Sunday evening like this, around ten pm, when more sensible or less reckless folks were already fast asleep, it seemed like this would be prime time for one of those swerving cliff-dives straight out of a Twilight Zone episode. Russ was either shivering because it was getting colder outside or because he was starting to frighten himself. He turned the heater on and a rush of warm air came huffing from the vents. Right when the darkness of the night and the quiet desolation began to cross the line from relaxing to erie, a crash rang out from the passenger seat.

"Son of a bitch!" Richie hollered. "Shit! Aaaaaaaa!" He moaned. He reeled his hand in tight to his chest and clamped it under his arm. "God damn it that hurt!" He took the hand back out and shook it.

Russ gripped the wheel and locked his shoulders tight. The car hadn't bucked an inch. Thank god his reaction had been to brace up instead of flinch. "Jesus Christ!" Russ shouted. "What the hell happened?"

Richie had the right ridge of his hand all the way into his mouth. He was gumming down on it like a sandwich. "I clipped the window when I went to chuck the smoke out," he said, slobbering and grumbling through his fingers.

Russ looked across at the window. A hairline crack had already begun to etch its way down the center of the pane. "Jesus," Russ said. "You broke my window."

"I'm sorry," Richie said. He could barely speak through the hand wedged in his lips. "Does it matter that I also broke my fucking hand?"

"Are you all right?" Russ said.

"Don't worry about me," Richie said, "you've got your window to think about."

"Oh come on," Russ said. "You're not dying."

"Okay, doc. If you say so."

"Man, whatever," Russ said.

Richie shook his hand some more and groaned. He kept cradling the injured paw in his lap then lifting it and flexing it in front of his face. He raised it up toward the ceiling and held it out the window, seeing if he could locate any visible damage against the dim moonlight. Russ didn't want to look away from the road for too long, but he did notice that the hand looked even fatter and pinker than usual. After a few moments, when Richie had finished inspecting the whole moist and fleshy appendage, he put the hand back on the armrest and started to laugh. Russ laughed too.

"That was some really weird shit," Richie said.

"I've never seen anything like that before," Russ said.

"Figures," Richie laughed. "We always get into some weird shit, don't we?"

Russ laughed. "Hell yes we do," he said. And they did. Over the last ten or eleven years, Russ figured they'd seen and done just about every weird thing there was to do in Wellton County.

Richie leaned down and flipped the radio on with his good hand. It was one of those stereo models that only exist in cars manufactured before 2010. All of the numbers and symbols on all of the buttons were worn away except the little triangular insignia on the eject one that served as the lever for both the CD and cassette tape functions. Maybe they didn't include enough bulbs back in 2007 either because the spotty blue lights on the dashboard were so faint and fuzzy that it was hard to tell what gear they were driving in. Tom Petty came on. "American Girl." Of course Tom Petty was on. Russ and Richie had once joked that at any given time in any town in America, some radio station was playing a Tom Petty song. They seemed to be on an endless loop, cycling through the atmosphere. Richie left it on, and for a little while they were silent again.

When the road straightened out, Russ chanced a longer look at the window. The crack was deep and jagged. It was hard to tell while he was driving, but it looked like the glass had been bent, almost like a fold, down the center of it. How could a single finger do that? How was that even possible? It was crazy, but Russ probably shouldn't have been that surprised. Everything about Richie was oversized, calloused and steely firm. He had the type of teeth and throat that could handle taking barroom bets, biting and swallowing shards of shot glass in one gulp. And outside Brogans Tap, late at night when he'd taken his wild screeds a little too far, he'd once displayed a back that could withstand a blow to the spine from a baseball bat. Why couldn't his finger break a car window? In high school, the football coach begged him to come out for the team, and Richie agreed to try. His giant legs and iron shoulders made for a perfect offensive lineman, and everyone could tell from only a few practices that he had what it took. The only things that could stop him were his constant absences from class and his penchant for coming to school blitzed.

Out on 422, once the road had opened up and there were enough lampposts strung together to illuminate the passing cornfields and dairy farms, Richie reached into his jacket again and this time he pulled out his flask. Lord only knew what else he kept in the flaps of that dirty thing. He took a hefty pull from the tall and clinking cylinder. This was his "gran-daddy" receptacle; the one he usually filled with Banker's Club whiskey and reserved for long nights of heavy drinking. He owned other smaller, less weighty vessels for his liquor, and Russ wondered why he'd brought this one along for such a short trip. They were only going to pick up another batch of cheap weed from the basketball courts up on Valley View hill. They called it the "skrimp," partly because the quality was so shabby, but also because Russ had one time swore that it smelled like sea-food. They passed the Penn Square shopping center, a sprawling concrete island filled with abandoned strip malls and a deserted grocery store. The only place still in business was a small gun and ammo shop in the far back corner of the lot. All of the lights had been left on inside so that drivers passing by could see the shotguns hanging in the window like polished jewelry, the perfect gift for romance. The statement seemed to be that no matter what the time, no matter what the occasion, there would always be someone home at Pete's Pistol Emporium.

"Look," Richie said, squeezing the flask back inside his pocket. "Check this out." He pointed up ahead, maybe eighty yards or so, to a large glowing billboard outside the steep entrance to Valley View. "They must have put that shit up like last night."

"Yeah, damn," Russ said. "That's huge."

As they got closer the enormous sign came more into focus. The structures that held thing aloft must have been thirty feet alone. The advertisement was forty feet wide and twenty feet high, lit up by two massive bulbs hooked to the lower scaffolding. The surface was shiny but dark, the figures somehow rising out from some ominous shadow, floating on a black pond. A towering woman stood over a withered man laid out on a wooden bed; a soiled quilt pulled all the way up to his emaciated face. Gathered at the sides of the bed were a group of young kids, presumably the man's many children. Over their heads, in bright white letters, it read: "E. Coli bacteria will knock you flat." At the bottom right corner was a logo, a vacant red circle with a line through it, and under that the words: Council for National Safety.

"What a load of trash," Richie said.

"What?" Russ said. "E. Coli or the billboard?"

"Yes," he said. He rolled his window down another inch and spat a wad of phlegm out onto the pavement. "All of the questions. Everything. Yes. Why is it here in Wellton? Why is it right outside the entrance to Valley View? Who paid for it? Why is the family black?"

"I don't know. I might not have even noticed the thing if you hadn't said something," Russ said.

"How many times have you ever gotten E. Coli poisoning?" Richie asked.

"Not counting the times I've had to clean up all of your shitty messes?"

"What?"

"Isn't E. Coli caused by contact with feces?"

"Wait, what?" Richie said. "You're an asshole."

"Come on. That was a good joke," Russ said.

Richie shook his head. He tried to roll his window back up, but it wouldn't work with the split down the middle. "You're still an ass hole," he said. "You know my mom and I like watching horror movies, right? We watch it for entertainment purposes. My neighbor, Joe, you met him before, the one with the big muttonchop sideburns, he watches horror, too. The doofus calls me over the other night and shows me that he bought four separate locks to bolt his door shut at night." He was still grappling with the window, trying to get it to budge. It wasn't cooperating. "The poor dude is watching that shit like he's researching for real life."

"A law and order guy, huh?" Russ said.

"Never mind." He was in a wrestling match against the window, and he was losing. "I'm trying to pop it back into shape," he said. It was hard going with his left hand. He was trying to yank the top part up with his injured right one.

"Look at what you've done to my beautiful car," Russ said.

"Dude, will you slow down?"

"Oh, shit," Russ said. He pressed down hard on the brake, veering into a shallow ditch, skidding into the narrow lane behind the laundromat. A plume of dust and debris sailed into the air before wafting down onto the windshield.

"Jesus, you could have killed us," Richie said.

"Would you let go of the window? You're going to rip the thing clean out of the frame?"

"If you would stop swerving all over the road maybe I wouldn't have to cling to the fucker for dear life."

"Well, you've got me staring up at billboards and thinking about shit borne diseases..." Russ trailed off. "Jesus, we are tense," he said. "We need to get to that weed."

Richie let go of the window and flopped back hard in his seat with a sigh. "I think you're right," he said. "I feel really amped up for some reason." He pulled the flask back out and took another swig.

The entrance to Valley View was concealed behind a 24-hour laundromat called The Washing Well. The way it was positioned right in front of the lane, sort of blocking the path, it always reminded Russ of some welcoming center at the gates of hell. As many times as they'd driven past it on their way up the hill, there'd never been more than one person inside. Tonight was no different - one slumped and drowsy man with a hooded sweatshirt pulled over his head. Maybe it was the same guy every time, the night watchman or maybe some mentally deficient shut-in comforted by the gentle whir of washing machines. He wasn't sure which scenario was more depressing. It was getting colder outside. Russ rolled his window all the way up and cranked the heater higher.

The ascent up Valley View Drive, much like the laundromat at its base, was foreboding. For starters, the road was hardly wide enough for a single vehicle. Heaven help the person who came face to face with another driver coming down the opposite direction. It was a straight incline from bottom to top without any plateau before the summit. It wasn't steep enough to necessitate four-wheel drive, but it was elevated enough to make the climb difficult for a junky car with two bald tires and the added weight of a wounded grizzly bear in the passenger seat. Aside from the grinding of the engine, the only other sound was that of the loose gravel sputtering out under the wheels. A few leaning shacks and neglected sheds, set off in the scruffy brush, marked the sides of the route like rustic landmarks. The whole process of reaching Valley View was a journey into the lives of a forgotten population. Russ had lived in Wellton fifteen years before he even knew the place existed, and he was certain there were hundreds more like him, citizens of the lowland walking around without the onerous knowledge of a forsaken trailer park on the hill, the lost city of Valley View.

At the top of the quarter-mile slope there was a wrought iron arch and through that crooked, rusty mouth a steady line of gray rectangular crates spaced evenly by plastic planter boxes and busted lawn ornaments. A woman in a fluffy blue bathrobe, her white hair kinking loose from their curlers and one broken slipper dragging behind her, shuffled to her mailbox. Russ screeched to a stop, watching as she opened the lid of the box and extracted something from inside. Whatever she retrieved was small enough to slip into the pocket of her robe. As she turned to go back inside her trailer, the robe flapped open to reveal a mess of purple and red splotches across her bare and wrinkled chest. Her backside was raw and uncovered too. The dappled line of flesh from her waist to her thigh was blue from the chilly air. Richie recoiled, made a hissing sound through his clenched teeth.

"Oooooooo, no," he moaned, averting his eyes. "No, no, no."

"Yeah," Russ said, "nobody wants to see that."

Wrapping the robe back over her breasts, the woman mounted her wooden steps and disappeared inside her single-wide. If she noticed them at all, there was no indication. This was nothing out of the ordinary for her, Russ thought, fetching some mysterious package from the mailbox while a car's bright lights bore down on her late at night was part of her evening routine. In her experience nobody observing had ever cared enough to check in on her suspect wanderings. Why would they start now?

The drive past the main bank of trailers always had a depraved and eerie quality, young boys clustered outside on wobbly porches drinking and smoking, middle-aged women sauntering down the side of the road with bare legs and skimpy tops covered by knockoff fur coats, advertising their haggard bodies. One had to anesthetize the senses against heartbreak and repulsion in order to reach the already nefarious destination. And how many people, Russ wondered, all over the globe right now were performing similar acts of sensual numbing in order to accomplish their shameful deeds? It wasn't just for the poor and desultory in Wellton, but the opulent set too, the loaded magnates dwelling on different hills in distant lands.

"They are out in full effect tonight," Richie said.

"No doubt," Russ said. He tightened his grip on the steering wheel, fighting back the urge to even blink. You had to drive extra slowly in order to account for drunk people walking out in front of your vehicle or rabid possums waddling across your path. These obstacles made the short trek all the more harrowing to accomplish.

The spot to find drugs was the basketball court on the far north side of the park. Judging by the drooping, netless rims, and the crumbling, weed-choked asphalt, the residents had given up on maintaining the surface for athletics and turned it over to the dope-dealing crew long ago. As with just about every other plot in the vicinity, if anyone was seeking refuge from their stormy lives, they'd need to look elsewhere. It wasn't difficult to locate the juveniles peddling their goods. You simply crept up to the chain-link fence and flashed your high-beams. In a matter of seconds, one of the scruffy high school kids would come out from behind the nearest trailer and approach your window. Tonight it was a lanky, chalk-faced kid with sagging jeans and a halting stride who came to the driver's side and peered inside. He had no coat on but instead wore only a pair of black cotton gloves and a black beanie hat pulled down far over his ears.

"What you need?" he said. Half of his bony body was angled toward the window and the other half aimed at the street for a quick getaway.

"One ounce of the green," Russ said.

"I got you," the boy said. If Russ had to guess, he'd say he was around seventeen or eighteen. There was enough beard growth along his pale jawline to signal that he was well into puberty but not so much to determine if he had finished it. He reached inside his jeans pocket, and when he did his pants sunk so low on his hips that Russ worried they might just slip all the way to the ground.

"Aye!" Richie said from the passenger seat. It was jarring enough to make both Russ and the boy do a double-take. His tone wasn't aggressive, but it was barbed enough to make you pay attention. You didn't ignore a guy like Richie when he spoke like that.

"What up?" the boy said.

"I have a question for you," Richie said.

The boy hiked his pants back up to his waist and darted a look over his shoulder then bent back inside the window. "Yeah?" he said.

Richie leaned over the gear shifter so that he was almost in Russ's lap. "Do you trust us?"

The boy took a step back. He narrowed his eyes and pivoted toward the trailer he had come from. Russ reached over and whacked Richie on the shoulder. "What are you doing, man?"

"Yo!" Richie shouted after the boy. "Don't worry," he said. "We mean no harm. For real. I promise." He put both of his hands in the air. He pulled the sides of his coat open to show that he didn't have anything on him. "I just want to talk."

"Talk?" The boy said. "What you mean?"

"Talk," Richie said. "Just talk. That's all."

Russ looked at the boy and shrugged. "It's cool," he said. "You don't have to."

"Are you guys cops?" The boy asked. He crammed the drugs back deep into his pocket and prepared himself to run. "You have to tell me," he said.

"We're not cops!" they both said at the same time. Russ gave Richie another confused look. "What are you doing?" he whispered.

The boy came back to the car slowly. He put both hands in his pockets and craned forward. "What you on? What up?" he asked again.

"I just asked if you trust us," Richie said.

"I don't know man," he said.

"My name is Richie. This is Russ. What's your name?"

"Dude, why you doing this?"

"Nobody ever asked your name before?" Richie said.

"Nah, Gee. Nobody ever asked me that."

"So you do illegal stuff for people without even knowing their names?" Richie asked.

The boy straightened up. He shook his head, clicked his tongue. "Man, get yo broke ass…" he said. "You want the shit or nah?"

"Dude, are you drunk?" Russ asked Richie.

"No," Richie said. "I mean, not yet. Hey, do you want some whiskey?" he asked the boy. He pulled the flask out of his pocket and held it up for the boy to see. "It's Banker's Club."

The boy laughed. "You is crazy, Gee."

"Is it crazy to want to get to know the guy who you're doing criminal business with? We don't know each other. How are we supposed to trust one another? I want to get to know you."

"What you want from me?" The boy asked.

"Your time."

"Shit, I can't just stand here all night and chat, bro."

Richie sat back in his seat. He stretched his arm around and popped the lock open to the back door. "Get in."

"Are you for real right now?" Russ asked.

"I'm totally for real. Look," he said to the boy. "You must be cold without a coat on. We have the heat on in here. Just hop in for a few minutes and we'll go for a ride. You can have a couple pulls from the whiskey, take a little break, and we'll have you back here in a few minutes."

The boy was considering the offer. Russ could tell he was interested, something about the way he kept shaking his head but also moving closer at the same time. It was clear he'd never been invited to get into anyone's car before. The smirk that was forming on his lips along with his loosening posture and forward progress, told Russ that he was leaning toward getting in. "You cool with this?" the boy asked Russ. He cupped his hands over his mouth and blew into them.

Russ shook his head, not so much to say no exactly, but more to just let the idea lodge into his brain. "Shit, I don't know." He looked over at Richie.

"It's fine," Richie said. "Let's be adventurous." He put one of his big bear claws on the back of Russ's neck and squeezed. It was hard to say how many times Richie had said something to this effect, but Russ did have to admit that at least half of the time it led to some kind of experience that was unforgettable and life-affirming. The other half of the time... well, it ended in bedlam.

Russ turned to the boy and nodded at the back door. "Get in," he said. What did he have to lose, really? He worked at a job that bored the piss out of him, and if he woke up late in the morning and lost the position, he could find another dead-end job that was just as good. What he couldn't do was find himself in this situation again. Damn it if he wasn't starting to think the way Richie thought. He was wearing off on him.

The kid opened the creaky door and swung it shut. Richie turned around and offered his hand. "Richie," he said.

"Willy," the boy said.

"That's more like it," Richie said. He took a drink from his flask and passed it back to Willy.

Willy tilted the flask back and took a gulp. "Thanks, man." He handed it back to Richie then wiggled in his seat, trying to get warm. He scooted back and forth for a while, anxious to find some familiar level of comfort in a foreign setting.

"You go to Wellton High?" Richie asked.

"Sort of," Willy said.

"Sort of?" Richie asked.

"I mean, I'm on a roster somewhere, but do I go? Not really."

Richie and Russ laughed. "We know how that goes," Russ said. "Class of 2011 right here. Best and brightest."

"Ha!" Willy said. "No doubt."

He looked exactly like all of the Valley View kids that Russ and Richie had gone to school with years ago. He had the same cagey look in his eyes, the same dismissive, jaded tone and the same disheveled marks of famine in his faded clothes and scraggy skin. No doubt they still performed the same Valley View gang signs in the locker rooms and cafeterias when no teachers were watching – both thumbs and forefingers pointed straight up like double Vs. They called themselves "Dub-V Posse" for short. And Russ was sure that all of the other kids still labeled them outsiders, claiming they "acted black" or "looked like white hood rats." As it turned out they were all just acting like kids in poverty, too tormented and disenfranchised to do anything other than feign toughness to save face or cover for the trauma lying just beneath the surface. It was the same boyish and self-destructive posturing that could be found in any poor community in the country, no matter the color.

Russ shifted into drive and pulled out onto the dirt road. "Where to?" He asked. "Do you have a tour you take people on if they are new in town?"

"Shit," Willy said. "This is it. What you see is what you get. Just keep taking right turns when you see them. The whole place is one big fucked up rectangle."

"Why are there so many people still awake?" Richie asked.

"I mean, why not?" Willy said. "Nobody really has a job or they work part-time, some late shift that won't start until four or five o'clock anyway. You gotta do something to entertain yourself."

"You have a lot of family that lives back here?" Russ asked. He was driving about five miles an hour, which was really hard to keep up. He was worried that if he drove too fast their trip would be over too soon, and now that things were moving along and nothing sinister had happened yet, he was starting to enjoy the little adventure.

All of the surfaces were broken and rotting. The speed bumps were in pieces and the speed limit signs were so tarnished and bleached it was hard to read them.

"I don't really know my family," Willy said. "I mean, I have a half-sister who lives here, and I have an uncle, but I don't know anybody from my dad's side, and my mom's in jail."

"Aw, man," Russ said, "that sucks. I'm sorry, dude."

"Yeah," Willy said. "It's trash."

Richie took another sip from his flask and passed it back to Willy again. "But you know a lot of people here, at Valley View I mean?"

Willy took the flask and drank. "Well, yeah, I mean I've lived here pretty much my whole life and there's only like fifty or sixty people left up here."

"Do you know who killed Kirby Baxter?" Richie asked.

"Whoa, fuck," Willy said. He flung back against the seat and put his hands up in the air. "What kind of question is that, bro? Jesus, I knew you guys were narcs. I fucking knew it. Let me out. Pull over." He started trying to open up the back door but the automatic locks were on and with his mind racing and his nerves jumping all over the place he couldn't open it.

"Hold on, hold on," Russ said. He pulled to the side of the road and stopped the car. "Jesus, Richie. What the fuck?"

"I'm just asking," Richie said.

"I don't know nothing about shit!" Willy said. "Let me out of here."

"Calm down," Richie said, "take it easy."

"What are you the fucking FBI or some shit now?" Russ said.

"Relax," Richie said. He turned around in his seat and held up both hands to show him they were empty. "Chill, okay. Chill out. I already told you that we weren't looking for trouble."

"Don't ask me fucked up questions like that," Willy said. He stopped fumbling with the door and sat back against the seat. He folded his arms over his chest and frowned. He was pouting. Christ, he was just a kid, Russ thought. This was nuts.

"I'm sorry," Richie said. "I'm sorry. Did you know him. You knew Kirby?"

"Yeah, I fucking knew him. I told you I know everyone."

Russ put his hands over his face and sighed. He put his head down on the steering wheel.

"Russ saw the murder," Richie said.

"Richie!" Russ hollered into the wheel.

"What?" Willy snapped. He slammed back against the seat as though shoved. The shock stiffened him, pasted him there against the cushion. "Fuck. That's horrible. Oh, Jesus," he whispered.

"What?" Richie said. "Will everyone just get a grip. What's so wrong with trying to find out who killed Kirby Baxter? He seemed like a good kid. I feel bad for him and his family."

"He was a good kid," Willy said. "He was about the only fucking good kid we had up here."

"See," Richie said. He turned to look over at Russ's prostrate form leaning against the steering wheel. He put a hand on his shoulder.

"Don't," Russ said, shirking the hand away. Richie removed his hand.

"You saw the murder?" Willy asked.

"I don't want to talk about it," Russ said.

"Well, why did we come here then?" Richie asked.

Russ raised his head. He pounded the steering wheel with his palm. "We came up here to get some fucking bud, ass hole! We came up here to get high, remember?" He spun away from Richie and stared out the window. "Unbelievable," he said. "You thought I came up here to track down Kirby Baxter's killer? Jesus. You're out of your mind."

"I thought we'd kill two birds with one stone," Richie said. "Sorry. That was a bad choice of words."

Willy took his hat off and ran his hand through his greasy hair. "We don't know what happened. None of us do. There was a kid who used to live here named Owen Cummings, and now he don't live here no more. The kid was insane. I mean psychotic. Totally fucked up. He used to torture cats and kill birds and shit. One time, somehow, he put one of those Alka Seltzer tabs in the stomach of a fucking pigeon and the thing exploded. It was gruesome, Gee."

"You think it could have been him?" Russ asked.

"Hell yeah, it could have been him."

"Have you told the police?" Russ asked.

"Fuck no. You gotta be out yo mind to trick on somebody around here. That kid's family was a bunch of clucks. His dad had all these American flags up everywhere. One on his roof, one on his pickup truck, one on his mailbox. He had an American flag bandana that he wore every fucking day. He had a confederate flag, too. He had it hanging in the living room. You could see that shit clear as day. He left the curtains open twenty-four-seven. Motherfucker was proud of that shit."

"You think it was a race thing," Richie said.

"Most likely," Willy said. "It was really fucked up." He put his hat in his lap and slouched down in the seat. "Kirby was different. I mean, he wasn't like everyone else. He was cool with everyone, Gee. Laid back cat. He knew how to talk to people. It was like he had this way of making you feel at ease. He'd just come right up to you, and before you could even flex or decide if you liked the brother or not, he'd shake your hand. He did it to everyone, and then he'd talk to you, man, you know? Like get to know you and shit. He asked questions and he listened… I don't know, man. Shit was sad."

"People don't listen around here, do they?" Richie asked.

"Kirby had a way of getting around that, too," Willy said. "He had this thing he'd do where he'd go around yelling, 'Everybody out of the pool!' Anytime there was a threat coming from the cops or a rival gang or a drunk dad who was on the loose… And he had no real alliances, dude. He didn't even have anybody he was really riding with, like specifically. He would do it for anyone. Everyone! He saw trouble coming, he'd shout it out. 'Everybody out of the pool!' People would listen to that, man. People listened to Kirby." Willy shook his head. He stuck his elbow out his open window and gazed out over all of the dusty, sun-scorched roofs lining the distance. "Guess nobody was looking out for him the way he was looking out for us."

When Willy stopped talking Russ realized that he had been nodding his head over and over again for the past few minutes, striking his forehead lightly on the steering wheel each time. "Poor kid," he said.

"And you never saw that Cummings family again?" Richie asked. Willy didn't answer. Just shook his head no.

"Mental health mixed with squalor mixed with ignorance. That shit is no joke," Russ was mumbling to himself. "That shit will get you every time."

The three of them sat there for a few seconds in silence, each nodding and processing in their own particular way. After a while a large brown-skinned man with a ponytail, maybe Native American, with no shirt on stumbled past the car. He was talking to himself as he rocked from side to side. If he hadn't grabbed hold of the front hood as he clattered past he'd have definitely gone down. He was wearing two sets of sweatpants and one pair of ripped sandals. The hair was what made him look Native American. There were some kind of plastic beads knotted in his long, brambly braid. His belly was so round and bloated at the bottom that it looked as if he'd swallowed a beach ball.

"Exhibit A," Richie said. They watched as he tripped over his own feet and nearly went down again in the cold mud by the side of the road. He eventually righted himself, cursing and swinging his arms the whole time. They followed his swaying movements as he ambled into the darkness.

"That's Pablo," Willy said. "He good. He don't harm nobody."

Russ shifted back into gear and tapped the accelerator. He maneuvered carefully back onto the path and continued along at a crawling pace. "Hey, Willy," Russ said.

"Yeah?"

"You mind rolling us up some of that marijuana back there so we can mellow out a little bit?"

"For sure," Willy said. "No doubt."

Richie reached into the glove box and tossed him some rolling papers. They passed the flask back and forth and took their time driving around the park while Willy rolled the joint. By the time they got back to the basketball courts, Willy was sealing the joint, sliding it through his lips and twisting the ends shut.

"She's ready," Willy said. He started to pass it up to Russ, but Russ stopped him.

"You first, man," Russ said. "You do the honors."

Willy fished a lighter out of his jeans and sparked it up. He passed it to Russ and Russ passed it to Richie. The flask followed the joint around the car in a rhythmic pattern so that it started to almost feel like they were playing a game. Russ passed on his turn several times, not wanting to get too tipsy before his drive back home. Richie took the biggest gulps and drags, while Willy took courteous little swigs and puffs, still trying to unwind. The items made their tranquil rotation until the cab was filled with a haze of gray smoke and all of them felt good and baked. Russ rolled down his window to let some air in and the smoke seeped out into the night. It was warmer outside now. A mild, tepid breeze swept through the car, the kind that often foretells a coming storm. The whole park was asleep now. The only noise outside was the soft purring of crickets and some distant cars passing by down in the hollow. It was a clear night with a half-moon and all the stars seemed endless and undying in a way that made you feel a little less hopeless about the planet.

Richie lit a cigarette, then offered one to Willy. He leaned forward over the seats and took it. "What happened to your mom?" Richie asked.

"You don't quit, do you, Richie?" Russ asked.

"It's okay," Willy said, taking a drag of his smoke. He slumped back against the seat and draped his arms over the backrest. He blew a puff of smoke up at the ceiling. "She got arrested for child endangerment," he said.

Russ shot Richie a threatening look. Richie caught it, hesitating before he spoke "So," Richie said, "did she… Wait, was it because… could you say more about that?"

"You know my little half-sister, the one I mentioned before?" Willy said.

"Yeah," Richie said.

"She left her in the car."

"In the car?" Russ said.

"Like overnight?" Richie asked.

"Christ, Richie," Russ said.

"What? What now?"

"For about ten minutes," Willy said. He inched forward on the seat and ashed out the window.

"No way," Richie said. "Seriously?"

"Seriously," Willy said. "Ten minutes. She stopped at the pharmacy to grab her heart meds. They called and said it was waiting for her. When she parked the car Jessica, that's my two-year-old sister, she was fast asleep in her car seat in the back. It had taken her all day to finally nap. She'd been up the whole night before with an earache and a fever. My mom hadn't slept in about two days. Her heart's bad. My mom's got extremely high blood pressure, and she was having a bit of a fit. Her heart starts racing. She needed her meds."

"Of course she needs them. She must have been freaking out," Richie said.

"Exactly," Willy said.

"They can arrest you for that?" Russ asked.

"Apparently so," Willy said. "You know what else they can do?" he asked.

"What?" Richie said. "Don't tell me..."

"They can smash your car window and take your baby," Willy said.

"Get the fuck out," Richie said.

"No," Russ said. "They can do that?"

"They have this little tool, it's like a mini ice pick," Willy said.

"They have a special tool for breaking car windows to save babies that don't need saving?" Russ asked.

"It's small enough to fit on a keychain. I think a random woman, like a regular mom from the sticks somewhere in Louisiana or something invented it. It has a name. I forget what it's called..."

"Of course she did," Richie said. He flicked his cigarette out the window with extreme force. "That's fucked up," he said.

"When my mom got back out to the car her window was broken, a cop was holding Jessica, who was screaming with fear, and another officer was waiting to arrest her ass."

"I'm sorry," Russ said. "That is ridiculous."

"My mom loves Jessica," Willy said.

"Of course," Richie said. "How much time did she get?"

"Three months," Willy said.

"No, that's too much," Russ said.

"That's way too much," Richie said.

"Rescue Me," Willy said.

"Huh?" Richie said.

"Rescue Me. That's what that device was called that broke my mom's car window."

"Like a baby crying out, calling out to the void..." Richie said. "I love that. And I hate it."

"That's warped," Russ said.

"For sure," Willy said.

For a few moments, everyone sat in the stillness left behind by the story. Russ and Richie stared blankly out the windshield. Russ wanted to ask Willy what he was doing now, where he was staying while his mom served her sentence, but he was too scared or sad, he didn't know which one. He wasn't sure he wanted to know the answer. Willy rested his head against the window, trying to cool off or maybe freeze his harried mind. Richie started quietly talking to himself, mumbling something under his breath.

"What's that?" Willy asked. He raised his head from the window.

"The billboard," Richie said. "It's just like the god damn billboard."

"What billboard?" Willy asked.

"You didn't see the billboard down at the entrance?"

"Nah. I barely leave here."

"There's a billboard down there of a man suffering through E.Coli," Richie said.

"What's that?" Willy asked.

"Exactly," Richie said. "Fucking exactly."

"What are you talking about, Richie?" Russ asked.

"I'm talking about bullshit. I'm talking about worrying about the wrong things. E.Coli? Babies being left it in cars? They're distractions. That's really what we need to be putting our time and energy into? We need prison sentences and billboards? It's all garbage. It's deception," Richie said. "It's… it's a hoax!"

"Yeah, but why?" Russ said.

"I don't get it," Willy said.

"What are the actual concerns that this county... Shit, this country, man... What are we really dealing with? What do you worry about the most, Willy?"

"I don't know. Food. Money. Stress. Drugs. My mom. My sister… um…"

"And do you see anybody putting up billboards for that?" Richie asked. "Do you see motherfuckers going to jail for taking jobs away from lower-class workers, bleeding them dry, taking food off their plates, causing dudes to turn to drug dealing to provide for their little fucking sisters? Where's the outrage for that?"

"Shit. I don't know," Willy said.

"Russ, how many overweight people… how many obese people have you seen since we got up here?"

"A lot," Russ said.

"You see any billboards about that? You see McDonald's CEO behind bars for pumping people full of chemicals and diseased meat? I bet less than a hundred kids per year die from being locked inside cars. I bet more motherfuckers get trampled by cows than die from E. Coli each year. How many poor bastards die every year because they can't afford the insulin for their diabetes? Hm? We don't care about that though, do we? No, no, look the other way. We want to punish the wrong people. That's what it is."

"Yeah," said Russ.

"Yeah," Willy said.

"If we keep putting all the blame on poor moms or black dads, nobody will look into the rich scum that is actually making everything worse. Sure, shine the spotlight on the peaks of Valley View and not the cliffs of Palo Alto. Fucking ass holes."

Everyone finished and extinguished their cigarettes. The flask was empty. Willy put his hat back on and just sat there for a while, thinking.

"Thanks for the chat, homies. I think I actually needed that."

"Anytime," Richie said.

"That was good," Russ said.

Willy opened the door. He put one foot out onto the dusty ground.

"Aye," Richie said. Willy stopped. Aside from the moon and a few stars, there was hardly a speck of light anywhere else to be found. In the darkness, Willy's face looked featureless and smudged, a blank hunk of stone. "It's not your fault," Richie said.

Willy nodded. He stepped out and shut the door behind him. Russ and Richie observed as he punched a hand into his pockets and pulled his pants up onto his waist. He headed for the long line of trailers, vanishing into the lightless crevice between two of them.

"I don't want to go home yet," Richie said.

Russ looked at the digital clock on the dashboard. It was just past twelve-thirty. "I can stay out for a few more minutes," Russ said. The damage was already done. "I mean, I guess. "What's the difference between twelve-thirty and one-thirty really, at this point?"

"One hour," Richie said. "It's still one hour."

"You can't turn it off, can you?" Richie said.

"Hey," Richie said. "Let's go looking for Owen."

"Oh come on, man. You heard Willy. He's long gone."

"I'm not sure though," Richie said. "Sometimes these dumb criminal types hide in plain sight. How far could they have gone?"

"Okay, it's my turn," Russ said. "They could have gone very far. They could have gone five hundred miles."

"I have an intuition," Richie said.

"You're drunk," Russ said.

"That's a type of intuition. You never heard of that?"

"We'll drive around for a few minutes, and then I need to go home."

"This is going to be fun," Richie said. "We're like investigators. P.I.s!" He sat up and spread his hands wide in front of the windshield like he was holding a banner. "Tracking bandits in Valley View. The woods of the soul," he said.

Russ didn't answer. He drove once around the park. Richie had his hands up to his eyes the whole time. He'd made circles of his fingers, and he was squinting through their curled holes as if he was using a pair of binoculars. The only thing he spotted, aside from a few stray hubcaps and empty oil cans, was an unpeeled banana in pristine condition. He laughed about the banana for five straight minutes. It was perfect, Richie said. Not even one brown spot on it yet. He wanted Russ to go back and get it. He pleaded. He was very drunk. When they had made the full rotation, Richie talked Russ into going around one more time. It wasn't worth arguing with Richie when he was this intoxicated. They passed by discarded bicycles and broken-down trucks with flat tires. They saw roving dogs scavenging for food and a hundred different US flags in countless forms and locations. Just as they were about to reach the road leading back down to civilization, Richie spotted something on the ground.

"Stop!" He yelled.

"What?" Russ said. He slammed on the breaks, and then right away felt stupid for how serious he'd taken the command. Once again he'd let Richie suck him into his lunacy.

"There!" he shouted, pointing to a loan fence post at the side of the lane with a jacket draped over the top.

"What about it?" asked Russ.

"Didn't you say the killer was wearing a black coat when he shot Kirby?"

"It's a black coat," Russ said.

"That's what I'm saying!"

"There are millions of black coats."

"Yes, but in Valley View?"

"Oh, for christ sake, Richie."

"I'm going to grab it."

"No," Russ said. "Don't."

"There could be fibers!" he said. He tore open the door and went charging for the coat as if someone was trying to chase him down. He grunted his way back inside the car and slammed the door. "Go, go, go!"

Richie refused to move. He kept the car in park and stared straight ahead.

"Let's go!" Richie said. "Come on. Move it!"

"I'm not doing this," Russ said.

"You are no fun," Richie said. He slapped the coat down on the floor mat and stomped his foot.

Russ thought about explaining to Richie about how insulting and insensitive it was to call this preposterous mission fun. He'd seen a horrifying thing, and his best friend wanted to turn it into a flippant game of cops and robbers. To be friends with Richie Hess was to overlook his juvenile bouts of madness and self-destruction and accentuate his moments of clarity and kindness. There were so many precarious calculations like that in life. Some people compute correctly, get lucky and live an exhilarating life, while others mismeasure, crash and perish. Deep down, Richie knew this better than anyone. He was the type of person who was perpetually rolling the dice, always betting on his own immortality.

"Let's go home," Russ said. He took his foot off the brake and began the unsteady descent down the hill. The whole drive down felt like navigating one long pothole.

"Suit yourself," Richie said. He tweezed his cell phone out of his pocket and held it up to the window. "Are you seeing this? This storm is going to be hella big."

Russ did see it. The sky had turned into a murky swirl of gray and silver. The clouds were drifting and churning across the vacant plain. A wind kicked up. The trees rippled and dappled in the breeze. Everything was turning the same color as the clouds, gray and white and twinkling, a warm shadow up top with a cold blue underbelly below.

"This is going to be a doozy," Richie said. He flipped the video mode on his phone and began recording. "Have I told you about my art project?" he asked.

"No," Russ said.

"It's called 'Rescue Me.' Yeah, that's it. Yeah, I just started the first one last week."

"Is that right?" Russ asked.

"It's a photo and video collage, like a documentary." He was still holding the phone up to the window, narrating his own movie. The car bumped and caromed along.

"A record," Russ said.

"Yes! Precisely!" Richie said. "A record. It's a record of all of the storms that have occurred or will have occurred over the last part of 2019."

"What are you doing with them?"

"I thought I'd compile them and maybe have a showing at the Halcyon."

"That would be cool," Russ said.

"Storms are getting worse," Richie said. "They're getting stronger, longer and more devastating. They're taking whole towns now, whole cities sometimes. God is getting angry. He's pissed, and every new storm is like another tantrum, a little peek at the coming apocalypse."

"That's bleak," Russ said.

"No doubt about it," Richie said. "Bleak, wrenching, terrifying. It won't go away just because we refuse to look at it or talk about something else instead. If I make this film at least people will have to look at it and see. They'll have to reckon with their own lack of interest. Their denial. Their complicity."

Russ looked over at Richie as he held the shaky camera up to the cracked and filmy window. There wasn't a chance that he was capturing much of anything. The only thing he was recording was his own scrapbook of drunken babble. Unlike Richie, who would have laughed at Russ under these same circumstances, Russ didn't have the heart. Maybe that was how they were able to stay together for so long. Their two shoddy hearts combined made one solid, pumping mass.

They were halfway down the hill. Richie was still recording but his determination was starting to wane. He propped his head against the window, steadied his elbow on the ledge and yawned. The valley looked almost majestic from this vantage point. The solid brick homes looked so plain and modest, as if to relish in their own austerity. It wasn't certain if the humble people of Wellton made the homes seem more simplistic or if the untouched homes themselves had worn off on the people, but it was clear they were a matching pair. The small businesses, too, content in their renouncing of all things showy or glamorous, made the whole vista seem quietly triumphant. There was the new suspension bridge running through campus, with it's blinking spires and nautical stanchions, that would have counted as impressive in just about any small town in the country. The flashing yellow bulbs encircling the theater marquee where Richie would never be welcome put Russ in a solemn but serene mood. Of course the tallest, most visible structures were the white and pointed steeples atop all the stoic, stained glass churches. Russ didn't think that was right, all the idolatry and idle luxuriance, but he'd come to terms with the reality years ago. Richie was a reality fighter, and would probably never let go, but he was still here too. These were cozy, familiar sights, even if neither one of them would ever admit it.

"This storm could topple every rattletrap home up here. Every single shoebox just blown to smithereens, obliterated, and nobody would even know it happened." Richie yawned one more time. He put his head in the crook of his arm and nestled into it. In a few minutes he was snoring. The phone was still running. It was clamped in his large hand, cradled by his upturned arm. Russ reached over. He tried sliding it from his palm, but even in repose his grip was too stiff and stubborn. After a few more tries, Russ decided to let him keep it. He hit the off button but left it there in his grasp, quaking and sweating all the way home.

5

So far, in the four days since Russ began work at Riegler Bank, he'd learned how every regular customer liked their bills counted, which type of corrosive cleaners *not* to use on the wooden countertop and, most importantly to Wayne, how to schedule days off at least three weeks in advance. Emergencies happened, Wayne said, and that was all right if it had to be, but vacations shouldn't just pop up out of thin air, at least not at Riegler. He was in charge of scheduling for the entire department, and getting everyone covered and clear each month was a "son-of-a-gun," Wayne said, which was also the closest Russ had ever heard him get to swearing.

Today, Wayne was showing him how to enter itemized transactions of five hundred dollars or more into the "Large Action Ledger" or the "LAL." Wayne had the glowing spreadsheet open on the screen, and he kept asking Russ to look closer and closer.

"There," Wayne said, tapping the screen "get in there. Right there. Do you see that line right there?"

"Yes," Russ said, his nose nearly touching the monitor now.

"Yeah?"

"Yes," Russ said, "I see it." He could see the line, yes. It was getting harder, though. They'd been staring at the same column for about ten minutes. His eyes hurt. What he could see more than anything was Wayne's gawky reflection in the smeared glass, his pasty white skin, fuzzy cheeks and two magnified eyes swimming behind the frames of his dense glasses.

"That cell, that cell right there," Wayne was saying, "that's the one that if you miss just one numeral, even one decimal, the whole sheet will be off. It'll be useless. Just pure frustration. Last time someone entered a transaction wrong in that column it took me about a week to figure out where the error went in."

"Wow," Russ said. "That sounds tedious."

"Ha! You got that right! Thank God for caffeine. I needed it that week." He raised the mug on the table beside him and waved it there.

"I think I'd need something stronger than that after that job."

"Haha! Well, I used to drink a beer from time to time, but I haven't been out for one in a while," Wayne said.

Finally, they were done staring. Wayne leaned back and Russ was quick to follow. Just the space alone to breathe more fully made a difference. His eyes felt bruised and tired. He stuck his knuckles deep into his sockets and rubbed.

"Why haven't you been out?" Russ asked.

"Well," Wayne said, "Clancy's used to be the place to be, you know?"

"No," Russ said, "it was?"

"Oh, yeah. You didn't know that?"

"I hardly ever go to Clancy's. My friends and I are always over at The Sundown."

"What's that? Where's Sundown?" Wayne asked.

"Wait," Russ said, "you never even heard of The Sundown?"

"No, I don't think so," Wayne said.

Russ didn't know how to respond to this. If The Sundown wasn't the most popular hangout for twenty-somethings in the entire county, Russ didn't know what was. Russ and Richie had drunk at every bar, grill and tavern within a wide radius, and without a doubt, The Sundown was the most widely known. Clancy's had a reputation for catering to an older crowd. It was in a backwoods part of town where they kept all the bingo parlors and VFW lodges. There was absolutely no nightlife around. If somebody wanted to lay low or listen to Hank Williams or maybe get a cold one with their grandfather, they showed up at Clancy's. The fact that Wayne didn't know Sundown but he knew Clancy's, it made Russ feel like they were living in two different worlds.

"Well, all right then," Russ said, "Go on. You were going to say why you don't go out anymore."

"Right," Wayne said. "Well, one night, maybe three months ago, my pal and I were sitting at the table in the back of Clancy's, you know the one, the one right against the window by the jukebox."

Russ tried to picture what he was talking about, but it had been more than a few years since he'd been in Clancy's. "I think so," he said.

"Yeah, well, we're sitting there, trying to eat our fries and burgers, when all of a sudden, out of nowhere, some big old bird comes soaring right into the window. Smack!" Wayne clapped his hands together to make the sound. He wheeled back in his chair and put his hands behind his head. The springs creaked under his swaying weight. "Scared the heck out of us! I nearly dropped my burger. Louis, my buddy, he screamed! I think he was traumatized. It was nuts! I haven't been back there since."

"A bird?" Russ said.

"Yeah, man. A huge thing! It might have been a chicken hawk or something, I don't know."

"Did it, like, start bleeding or screeching or flailing around all wild or something?" Russ asked.

"Who knows? I don't know. We weren't about to check. We just wanted to get out of there as soon as possible. Haven't been out since," he said, shaking his head. "That did it."

Russ nodded his head while Wayne shook his, and when he couldn't think of any other thing to say, he just kept nodding some more. He thought that if he sat and nodded for long enough, he might come up with a polite or humorous way to tell Wayne how odd and off-putting he thought the story was. It never came, so as the dueling head motions began winding down, the two of them just sat there in silence for a while. What could someone who had witnessed a murder and kept drinking say to someone who had seen a bird get injured by a window and give up for good?

Really, if a single bird could make Wayne give up on having fun for three whole months, Russ didn't want to venture any further down that line of thinking anyway. This wasn't the first instance where he and Wayne had been on opposite ends of the spectrum when it came to ideas about having a good time. They seemed to disagree on everything. And it wasn't like they were misconnecting in the obvious, familiar ways people do like chocolate versus vanilla ice cream or something. It was like one of them liked chocolate ice cream and the other preferred fried anchovies for dessert. At least that's how it seemed to Russ, and he knew he was the anchovies in the relationship. It must have felt the same way to Wayne. Just yesterday Wayne rattled off a list of his five favorite movies while Russ sat by stone-faced and bewildered. All of his favorite movies involved superheroes, explosions or fantasy worlds. The list started with Star Wars and finished with The Never Ending Story. It sounded like a list that a thirteen-year-old would write. Why were so many adults watching films and TV shows with dragons, capes or vampires? Russ didn't understand. He knew it was happening, that thirty and forty-year-olds were going to the theater on opening day of flicks like Aquaman, but he kept trying to pretend that it wasn't. If he admitted that everyone else had tastes in art or entertainment that made him nauseous, he'd have to acknowledge other snobby or elitist tendencies about himself. His were not Wellton approved perspectives. These were things that earned you names like snowflake or retard. The thing of it was, he really didn't feel pretentious at all, not deep down. He was just a normal guy. If you really thought about it, wasn't he being more down to earth than they were? He wanted to watch movies about ordinary people with common hardships. It comforted him to know that there were others out there going through the same stuff he was, like underemployment, heartbreak or crappy living conditions. For the two hours he sat and watched a realistic movie, he was not alone. Wasn't that the opposite of elitist? Sometimes Russ thought that people had their labels mixed up, backward and out of place. Being told to imagine immortal characters with laser eyes or glowing swords, did nothing to give him solace in a land filled with mortal, fallible souls. He just couldn't understand what was so great about make-believe. Here they all were living in one of the most fraught and volatile times in the history of the world. Come on, Russ thought. Reality isn't juicy or immersive enough for you? He didn't get it. A few nights ago he watched a documentary about how America's space program was costing over four trillion dollars a year. Meanwhile almost twenty percent of people living in the United States had slipped below the poverty line. That's the real zombie and alien shit that nobody wanted to see on the big screen, he guessed. Well, fuck them. Russ wanted to drop some of that weight on Wayne, make him answer for it, but he didn't have it in him. What was he going to do, ask him if he ever heard of Werner Herzog?

"Do you mind if I take my smoke break now?" Russ asked. It was the first words either of them had spoken in what seemed like a very long time. Wayne sat forward again and rolled his chair back over to the screen so he could check the time. It was almost ten o'clock.

"Now seems like a perfect time actually. The morning crowd has come and gone and the lunch brigade won't be here for another couple of hours," Wayne said.

"Great," Russ said. "I'll see you in a bit."

Wayne pulled the green Post It note with his dad's name on it off of the corner of the screen and walked toward the back offices.

Russ couldn't wait to get outside. He left his jacket behind in the breakroom. He had the cigarette halfway out of the pack before he even reached the door.

Opening the door to the parking lot, Russ had the sensation that he was escaping some great catastrophe. Had the bank gone whooshing up in flames behind him, he'd not have been the least bit surprised. He needed to wash the memory of the conversation out of his mind. That's what cigarettes were for. He often wondered what other people did to clear away bad thoughts or awkward situations without the aid of nicotine. He flicked his lighter. The sky was a soft blue and pink. It was warm enough to be outside without a coat, but Russ thought it excessive to see a man in shorts and a T-shirt washing his Ford pickup in the open garage across the street. The man had on a blue bandanna and was listening to country music.

"Well, fancy meeting you here," a woman's voice came from behind him. It was Natalie. She was carrying a plastic bag filled with food containers and a diet soda. She had a windbreaker on overtop a long dress. Her face looked fuller and shinier in the outdoor light.

"Hey," Russ said. "You went to go grab some lunch, I see."

"Yep," she said.

"Where'd you go?" Russ asked.

"Over to that new place on Willow Street. The Mexican place. Lupita's. Have you been yet?"

"Oh, right. No, I haven't. I've heard about it, though. Is it good?"

"They have this lunch special where you get two tacos, beans, rice and a salad for $7.99. Oh, and a soda," she said, holding up the bag. "It's enough for me to eat two lunches. I save some and put it in the fridge for tomorrow."

"That's nice," Russ said. "And it's good?"

"It's so much food. I can't eat it all in one sitting. Convenient, though. I won't have to bring or buy anything for tomorrow." She raised her left eyebrow, made a fish face with her lips.

"Oh, I get it," Russ said. "You're nice. You're a nice person."

"I like the idea of having more than just burgers and pizza in town," she said.

"Yeah," Russ said. "I agree. We needed another Mexican place in town. The Hacienda was alright, but it's been going downhill for awhile."

"I agree. I love Mexican food! I could use five places in town."

"Ha!" Russ said, "why not six?"

"Let's not get carried away," Natalie said. Russ laughed. He liked her. She was funny.

The guy in the garage turned up his radio. He moved to the front bumper and began swabbing it with a sudsy cloth. The frayed ends of his jean shorts dangled in the pool of water by his feet.

"So, how do you like the job so far?" Natalie asked.

"It's…" Russ paused. "Well, I mean, it's okay."

"Oh," Natalie said. She frowned. "You don't like it."

"No, no," Russ said.

"No, it's okay. Be honest."

"It's just that," Russ said, "well, I don't really understand what my job is exactly."

"What do you mean?"

"I mean, well, that's just it. I don't know what I mean."

"Like you aren't understanding the training?" Natalie said.

"Like I'm not *receiving* any training. Do you know what I'm saying?" said Russ.

"No," Natalie said, "you'll have to tell me more."

Russ sat down on the curb. "Do you want to sit down? Do you have a few minutes?"

Natalie looked at her watch. "I have a few." She sat down beside him, resting the bag between her long dress-covered knees.

"Wayne hasn't told me how to, like, help any customers," Russ said. He took a drag from his cigarette. He turned his head away from Natalie and blew the smoke out.

"Do you mean like how to deal with a tricky customer? One who has a big problem or something?"

"No, no! That's the thing. That's what I'm talking about. I know what to do if I get an irate customer. I know the set protocol for that."

"Okay," Natalie said, "so what do you still need?"

"Everything else! Like, okay, what do I do when a customer comes up to my window and asks to withdraw a hundred dollars?"

"You get it for him."

"Maybe that's a bad example," Russ said.

"It might have been," Natalie said.

"What if someone wants to cash their paycheck?"

"Is this a hypothetical question?"

"No! No, Natalie. This is what I'm trying to tell you. All I have the answers to are hypothetical questions. I know what to do if somebody tries to rob the place. I know how to check and double-check the books in case an employee is trying to steal from us. I can tell you what to do if there is something hazardous, a toxic chemical spill of some sort in the vestibule, say, or if a little kid throws up on the carpet. What I can't tell you how to do is deposit a birthday check from somebody's freaking grandpa!"

"That doesn't sound helpful."

"Yes, thank you! It's like Wayne's training me how to act in case a movie crew ever shows up and wants to film a bank heist picture. Or, like, how to survive if we ever find ourselves in a situation where the bank becomes a shelter during an apocalyptic outbreak of a deadly disease."

"That's not very practical," Natalie said.

"You think this is funny, don't you?" Russ said.

Natalie started to laugh, and once she started she couldn't stop. "I'm sorry," she said.

"No, by all means," Russ said. "Go ahead. Laugh it up. You're not the one who has to go to work every day with the knowledge that they can't explain their job."

"I'm so sorry," Natalie said again. She covered her mouth with her hand and finished laughing into it, then she took a deep breath and coughed. Russ liked that Natalie was the type of person who laughed easily. Life was too short, too absurd not to let out a good roar from time to time. He'd always been drawn to people who let their enthusiasm fly without any filters or apprehensions. Those were the type of people who had an adventurous heart, the people who were always up for a little mischief. Russ decided that while he was not physically attracted to Natalie, socially and emotionally speaking, they had potential to be great friends. "Okay, okay, I have my composure now," Natalie said, but a few seconds later the laughing started back up, and then she had to apologize all over again.

Russ finished his cigarette, but they were both still sitting there. The guy in the garage was working his cloth around the hubcaps now, singing along to whatever twangy tune was coming from the speakers.

"Do you mind if I ask you something?" Russ said.

"Ooo, I don't know," she said. "This sounds dangerous."

"You know that guy who came in last week to see you? Big guy. Long beard. Funny hat?"

"Yeah," Natalie said, "I remember." She seemed a little surprised to be conjuring up the moment again, but she was willing to go with it. She shook her head. "His name was Henry."

"Henry. Okay. He looked like a Henry."

"What's that supposed to mean?"

"Nothing. It doesn't mean anything other than what I just said. It's not a secret code or anything."

"All right." She put her hands in the air and shrugged.

"All right," Russ said. "What was his deal? It seemed like you two had weird tension or something. Was I picking up on that right or am I off?"

Natalie sighed. "You're not wrong necessarily," she said. "We had a little thing a few years back."

"A little thing?"

"He had a crush on me. Wait. Why am I telling you this?"

"I don't know," Russ said. "Maybe because there's nobody else around here you can tell or maybe because we both like Mexican food or we both like to laugh a lot?"

Natalie smiled. She shook her head and sighed again. "Right. Okay." She raised her eyebrows. "Are you sure you want to hear this?

"Never been more sure," Russ said. "You know me. It's me, Russ. Haha!" It was strange, but Russ already felt like they had known each other for a long time. There was an openness about her that made you feel you could talk about anything. She had that look, that freedom of spirit that Richie would have called "a twinkle in her eye." Richie would like Natalie.

"Right, right… All right." She gave him a look like he was a little daffy, but she went on anyways. "We worked together when I was a kindergarten teacher."

"You used to be a teacher?"

Natalie nodded. "Yep. For just a couple of years. I didn't like dealing with all of the nose bleeds and crying tantrums and poopy pants."

"Hazardous spills," Russ said.

"Exactly," she said. "Anyway, Henry was my assistant. He was getting his degree as an elementary teacher at the time, and he needed some hours in a classroom to get his certificate." She stops to gather her thoughts. She slides her hands across her dress, making a deep fold down the center of her thighs. "Anyway, everything was fine until Valentine's Day."

"Uh-oh," Russ said.

"What?"

"Nothing. It's a reflex," Russ said. "Classic setup."

"Oh," Natalie said, "I'm glad this is amusing you."

"Go on. I'm sorry."

Natalie bunched the flowing fabric of her dress in her fingers and slid the hem up above her ankles where Russ was surprised to find a pair of worn tennis shoes lying beneath. That was when Russ realized that the reserved quality and frowzy style he had noticed on the first day he met her was one of studious convenience. She was an ex-teacher. Of course. The plain attire could have helped to give her away, but also her patient and sweet demeanor. Russ could easily imagine a group of children pulling on those streaming dresses, wiping their noses and drying their tears in the folds. It all made sense now.

"So Valentine's Day comes and all of the kids are making these dorky, cute cards with like Snoopy and Mickey Mouse on the cover, and it's really sweet even if the kids are mostly grossed out by the cooties aspect. Well, Henry, Henry decided to give me one of these corny cards. He gives me this huge pink and red heart that he had cut out himself. It's all jagged and crooked and there's glue stains all over it. At first I think he's joking, but then I open it up. On the inside, spanning the whole space, he just wrote LOVE in enormous capital letters. It had all of this gold glitter all over it, and it was just… it really caught me off guard."

"Oh," Russ said. "Yeah, you weren't expecting it. That put you in a bad spot."

"No," Natalie said. "I mean, I knew he had a little something for me, but that seemed a bit much. I probably handled it wrong. He tried to explain how he was only going with the basic theme of the holiday, nothing mushy. He said he was making a paper version of one of those candy hearts."

"So that's what he was talking about that day when he said something about the heart. He said it wasn't about the heart or he didn't mean the heart that way or something like that… Jesus, and I thought he was talking about something medical or grotesque."

"Yeah," Natalie said. "Wait. What? You could hear us?"

"I was trying to," Russ said. "Wayne wouldn't be quiet."

"Eavesdropping on the first day," Natalie said. "Shame on you."

"I was so bored, and your little confrontation seemed like the most excitement I could possibly get in there."

"It wasn't really a confrontation," Natalie said.

"You didn't feel weird about him coming in like that?"

"Not really," she said. "I mean, I always sort of liked him. Things ended weird, but I always kind of wondered what happened to him."

"Wow. I did not pick up on that vibe. That adds even more intrigue to the situation. So, are you going to go out on a date with him?"

"I've been considering it, but I'm leaning toward no."

"That's what I was going to guess."

"Why?" Natalie asked. "What are you thinking?"

"You know. It's just that… He was a little… I don't know. Tell me what you think. Why are you leaning toward no?"

"The real hold up for me was always his beard," she said.

"His beard! That's the big thing? Really?"

"Yes! What? What are you getting at?"

"Nothing. Sorry. What is it about his beard?"

"It's too sharp and scratchy," she said. "One time, when we were both bending over a table to help a kid with this math problem, our faces touched and it felt like somebody had stabbed my cheek with a thumbtack. I'm surprised it didn't draw blood!"

"Well, a sharp beard has its drawbacks, sure. But what about his…" Russ had to stop and think. How would he put this? "What about his observations?"

"What do you mean by that?"

"I heard him. What he said when he first noticed you up at the window."

"Okay. So what?"

"He said, and I quote, 'You look different, but your breath smells just the same.'"

Natalie chuckled. "I forgot about that."

"How could you forget?"

"I don't know. It wasn't a big deal to me."

"But that couldn't have been the first or only thing he ever said like that."

"Why not?"

"The type of person who says something like that, he has other things, too. He's a type. There's a whole package. You tell someone, 'he's the type of guy who talks about your breath openly in public,' and people will go, 'Ooooh, I know that type.'"

Natalie laughed so hard that she stepped on her bag of food. It toppled over, and it took her some time to set it back upright again. "You are hilarious," she said.

"Am I?" Russ said. "That you notice. Humor is something that gets your attention?"

"You should really meet my friend, Darlene," Natalie said. "You're single, right? Are you single?"

"You assume," Russ said. "The funny guys are always single, right?"

"No, that's not what I meant. Oh, you and Darlene have to meet. She'll be here on Friday."

"I haven't even told you if I'm single yet."

"You will like her. We went to high school together in Lititz. Do you know Lititz?"

"I've heard of it. That's Amish country, right?"

"Yeah, but it's also home to some really kooky things too like the pretzel factory and the Wilbur Chocolate Store and a wolf sanctuary. That's what Darlene is like."

"She's like a wolf sanctuary?"

"Kind of," Natalie laughed. "She's kooky."

"And I'm kooky," Russ said.

Natalie nodded enthusiastically as she spoke. "Darlene goes to this really tiny art school in New York City. It's run by a bunch of hippies. I think it's called The Shill School or something like that."

"It can't be called The Shill," Russ said. "Like a fraud or a decoy? No."

"It was something like that," Natalie said. "Shelbington? I don't know. Anyway, she told me last night that she's taking a class called 'Body, Memory, Landscape.'"

"That sounds fascinating," Russ said.

"That makes sense to you?" Natalie said.

"Of course it does!" said Russ. "Planes of existence," he said.

"See!" Natalie shouted. "You two are perfect for each other!"

"Could be," Russ said.

Russ stared across the parking lot and thought about art schools in big cities. If he had one wish in life, it might be to go back to college again in someplace like New York City. He'd never even been to New York before, but in his mind it seemed like a place that would invite some offbeat rambler like himself in, his own Russ Sanctuary of sorts. A chill ran through him and he shivered. He couldn't tell if it was actually getting colder or if the guy in shorts across the street was just making him feel like it was. The guy was covered in the bucket water he was sloshing onto the truck. His socks were soaked. A puddle of green and pink soap leaked out around his white sneakers. A new country song had come on. It sounded just like the one before, heavy in jangly guitar and full of complaints.

"Everybody wants to go to heaven," Natalie said, breaking into song. She patted her hands on her knees and rocked back and forth. It took a second for Russ to realize that she was singing along to the song in the garage. The guy was singing too, stomping his foot as he ran a washcloth over the windshield. They were performing a duet together without even knowing it. "Have a mansion high above the clouds. Everybody want to go to heaven. But nobody want to go now!"

"You know all the words, huh?" Russ said.

"Yeah! Of course. You aren't a Kenny Chesney fan?"

"I've heard of him," Russ said.

"Holy mackerel, Russ!" Natalie said. She picked her bag up and started to stand from the curb. "How long have you actually lived in Wellton?"

"My whole life," Russ said.

"Your body might have been living here, but your mind…" Natalie trailed off. "Come on," she said. "We should be getting back in."

Russ stood up from the curb, clapping dirt and pebbles from his palms and wiping his pants clean. There wasn't a lot in life that was truer than what Natalie had just implied. They couldn't have been sitting there that long, but already Russ had nearly forgotten that he was working in the building that stood behind him and he needed to return at some point. He wondered how long he would have sat there thinking about nothing and everything and listening to country music as the guy hosed down his truck if someone hadn't interrupted him. When he was done having that thought he turned around and noticed Natalie had already gone inside with her things. It was almost 10:30.

6

On the walk to meet Daniel and Teresa, Russ practiced his tough-guy act. He'd once seen Richie turn around in a movie theater, put his arm over the seat, and tell a guy, "Why don't you take that chatter out to the fucking parking lot." He'd said it with a heightened volume and deep tone, but also with an air of nonchalance that made Russ want to live inside that bubble of bravado forever. There was a brief moment in which the stunned offender, a medium-sized man with a bald head and greasy cheeks, almost coughed out a response. But he couldn't find his way past the bracing gaze of Richie Hess. Russ couldn't see the look because Richie was facing away from him, but whatever it was had the power to halt a grown man in mid-sentence and steer him toward silence for the rest of the film. That was what Russ wanted to embody, that unnamable, unshakable quality of mettle. He tried imitating it in the way he pinned his shoulders back and tilted his stride forward. Maybe it was in the way you carried your weight up high and stood as tall as possible. The charade was just starting to feel a bit too absurd when he stepped sideways into a pothole and twisted his ankle. Not only was the mousy squeal that came from his mouth nothing close to macho, but it also jarred him out of character and back to reality. He hoped nobody had heard or seen his little debacle.

There was a sparrow up ahead on the sidewalk who seemed to be mocking him with his rapid chirping and cockeyed hopping, but no human witnesses. Russ tried shooing the bird away by kicking at it and waving his arms, but it only seemed to anger it into louder tweeting. Following several flailing attempts he was forced to walk around it, careful not to further ruffle its tiny scorn.

It was a bright and chilly day. He wore sunglasses and two heavy sweaters, both of which he kept trying to worm deeper inside. By the time he reached the next crosswalk his foot was hot and tingling. He pretended not to notice. This was not part of the plan.

When they spoke a few nights after their first encounter, Russ told Daniel that he couldn't find anything about a "mortality violation" written anywhere in any building codes or registries online. Daniel's response, one of detached acceptance, made it clear that he never expected him to find anything in the first place. The mission had been more of a test to see if he could trust Russ. When he was satisfied that he could he asked Russ to meet him and Teresa Saturday morning outside the Holcomb property again. Russ couldn't understand how he could be of any further use, but Daniel assured him that he was a valuable part of the next steps. Teresa and Dan had set up a second meeting with James Rolland, and they needed Russ along to act as a mediator. Dan's thought was that if a white man from the neighborhood was present, James would be less likely to toss around bogus reasons for denying them the property. It was difficult to explain, Russ tried telling them, but he probably wasn't the right type of white resident or enforcer they were picturing for the job. He had certain abnormalities that made him his own kind of alien around town. They were well aware, Daniel said. That was why he was perfect. James wouldn't know what to make of him. He could be anyone, they told Russ. You're a wild card, they told him. It didn't sound like bad logic, really. Russ figured it couldn't hurt much. Aside from the general discomfort surrounding the whole spectacle, the idea wasn't too bad. Russ had to admit that it was an intriguing plan, playing the role of Richie for a day, and he didn't have anything else to do. He agreed to meet them there at nine.

Russ could see the decaying remains of the Holcomb property up ahead on the left, and outside it Daniel and Teresa standing by, arms folded and mouths pursed, as though they'd been hired to pose there for a portrait in some restoration magazine. Teresa spotted Russ and waved. Daniel waved too, and then appeared to notice something funny. He guided Teresa's attention toward a pile of trinkets lying on the sidewalk one house down. He was pointing and laughing, and then Teresa began to laugh, too. Teresa covered her mouth, perhaps concerned that the object's owners were nearby, while Daniel refused to hide his hilarity. As Russ got closer the items came into focus, a heap of discarded scraps, likely leftover from a yard sale.

"Hey," Russ said, getting close enough to offer Daniel his hand. Daniel took it and shook, while Teresa came around the side and wrapped Russ in a hearty embrace. When she let go Daniel was still laughing. He couldn't stop. Teresa patted him on the back and tried shushing him. Daniel bent forward. He put his hands on his knees and tried to catch his breath. Teresa kept patting his back.

"It's okay," Teresa said. "Breathe. Breathe." She was wearing a new windbreaker, a bright purple one with a single hole for her head and no zipper in front. It was too big for her general frame, so that it looked like she'd pulled a parachute on over her head. When she noticed Russ looking at it, she grew self-conscious and stepped behind Daniel.

"What?" Russ said. "What's going on?"

"Why do you do it?" Daniel asked.

"Me?" Russ said. "Do what?"

"Americans," Daniel said.

"What do I do?" Russ said. "What do we do?"

"You put your old trash out on the sidewalk and ask strangers to clean it up for you."

Russ looked over at the objects where Dan had been pointing. Somebody had hand-painted a wooden sign that read: "Free Stuff" and leaned it up against an old set of roller skates. He smiled and shrugged.

"You have the broken rollers stakes. Then you have some chewed-up slippers, an old tire and a worn-out pair of swimming trunks with missing string."

"They are trying to be charitable," Russ said.

"They're being insulting," Daniel said. "That's not a sale, it's a bonfire."

"Okay," Teresa said, "shhhhhh. Take it easy."

"What is wrong with Americans?" Daniel asked. "They have such a backward way of offering support."

"They didn't do such things in Texas?" Russ asked.

"Oh, they did, only worse. The white people there used to dig out these cruddy gardens in the back of old parking lots, and then, then they'd invite us to come help maintain them for free! What a blessing! Community gardens, they call them. They were trying to save us! Is there anything more degrading?"

"Honey," Teresa said, "you should really keep your voice down." She kept looking over her shoulder, and the last time she did it she must not have liked what she saw because her shushing and back-patting began to take on a more frantic and urgent rhythm. This time Russ looked to see what she was panicking about. What he saw was a rather stocky man approaching, cutting across the street in their direction. His gait was clunky and heavy-footed, a lumberjack tromping through a forest.

"I don't know," Russ said, "I guess I see what you mean. You've lived here for a long time, right? Do you ever get used to it?" He was trying to stay calm, keeping one eye on Daniel and one on the man who was closing in behind Daniel.

"I was born here in the US," Daniel said, "but I was back and forth all of the time. That's why my English is a little choppy sometimes. Overall, I've spent more time in Mexico than in America. And Teresa, she was born in Mexico. She spent all of the 1990s there helping raise her nieces and nephews. She isn't a full citizen here yet. We might be the only Mexicans to ever sneak over the border going south. It's not as much of a rush!"

"Daniel," Teresa said, and this time she squeezed the back of his neck so hard that he let out a little groan, and when he turned around to see what was happening he was face to face with a rather large and burly man.

"You folks having fun here, are you?" The man's voice was low and gravelly. He wore a camouflage cap high on his domed head and gummed a wedge of chewing tobacco in his lower lip. Dark brown juice shot from his mouth and landed on the grass beside Russ's foot.

"Um, no," Teresa stuttered, "I mean yes. Sort of." She raked her palms down the front of her jeans to wipe the sweat clear, then stuck her hand out to the man. "My name is Teresa. This is my husband Daniel and this is Russ." The man accepted Teresa's and Daniel's hands but ignored Russ. He wasn't the one from which the man needed answers.

"What's your name?" The man asked.

"Teresa," she said. "Like I said… What's yours?"

"Caleb Moyer," the man said. "I live across the street." Caleb tossed a quick thumb over his right shoulder but didn't look to see where it landed. Teresa was just happy to know it wasn't the place with the junk set outside.

"Nice to meet you, Caleb," said Teresa.

"You knew the Holcombs?" Caleb asked.

"We didn't really know them, no," Teresa said.

"We know of them," Daniel said. "We know the story."

"I've seen you around here before," Caleb said. "Are you…" he paused. He raised the hat on his head just high enough to sneak a finger underneath for a brisk itching. "What's your angle? Are you looking for something?"

Russ could see it now. He connected the dots. This was the third time Daniel and Teresa had been sniffing around the property. James had been there once already, and now here was this sissy from around the way who was involved with whatever was going on, trying to force some issue. The word was out. The neighbors wanted answers about the business over at the old Holcomb residence, and Caleb was their colonel.

"We're looking for a home," Daniel said, "a place to live."

Caleb squeezed the hat back on top of his wide forehead. "You didn't know the Holcomb's," he said. Every gesture, every movement Caleb made struck Russ like a jab to the gut. Each act another glaring contrast in style and influence. Here was a guy who knew how to take on the job of bully, and each motion served as a reminder to Russ of his frailties, another mark against his own ineffectual ploy.

"What do you mean by that?" Daniel asked.

Caleb shook his head. A rattling chuckle came from deep in his belly. He spat another wad of chew onto the grass. A little of the splatter landed near to one of Teresa's sandals. Daniel put his hand in the center of her stomach and walked her back a few paces. Caleb looked at Russ and grinned, as though to further punctuate his undisputed authority.

"What do you know about the property?" Caleb wanted to know.

"Quite a bit, actually," Daniel said.

"More than they should need to," Russ said. This was his chance. Caleb seemed shocked that Russ had opened his mouth on the conversation. He snapped his head in Russ's direction, the way a dog might that notices his food bowl has been stolen. Russ was about to go on, spurned into action by his demeaning reception, when a flatbed truck rolled up to the curb beside them. The rumbling engine was cut, and a short man in a flannel shirt and muddy work boots climbed down from the driver's seat. The truck's tires were so tall and the man so short that he had to hang onto the door handle before plummeting onto the pavement. As the man got closer he appeared to get smaller, having placed himself in a position to be compared to the height of others nearby.

If the others knew him, and Russ assumed they did by their complete lack of reaction, nobody was letting on. "So you know about the pet cemetery, then?" Caleb asked. He looked from person to person, taking extra care to include the new arrival in his satisfied gaze. They definitely knew this man, Russ decided.

"What pet cemetery?" Daniel asked. He was now standing fully in front of Teresa so that she all but disappeared behind him.

Caleb chuckled. He grabbed hold of his brass belt buckle and yanked his pants up on his waist. "They don't know about the cemetery," he said, aiming his comments directly at the newcomer in the red flannel shirt. The man took up residence beside Caleb, his head about breast-high to his hulking stature.

"Why would we care about a pet cemetery?" Daniel asked. "What, there was a graveyard behind the house?"

"Yes," Caleb said, "quite an extensive one. The Holcomb's were not your ordinary family. They had their witchy ways, if you know what I mean."

Daniel turned and looked at Teresa then looked back at Caleb. "We don't care about a pet cemetery. That makes no difference to us."

"You should," said Caleb, spitting again. He was so pleased with himself. His belly shook with laughter as his elbow gently, covertly prodded the shorter man in the shoulder.

"Why?" Daniel said. He was leaning closer now so that Teresa had to take hold of his coat to prevent him from leaping forward.

"Well," the small man said. He looked up at Caleb then over at Daniel and back again. "Don't you Mexicans have a thing about spirits escaping the ground? You believe in ghost animals coming back to haunt the living. You've got a special day for it, don't you?"

"Now you listen here," Daniel said. Teresa tugged harder on his coat, and Russ stepped forward to block his path also.

"Who is this guy?" Russ asked, planting a hand in Daniel's midsection.

"That's James," Daniel said. "He's the inspector."

"We go back a ways," Caleb said.

"I bet you do," Daniel said, "back to those good old days, huh? Couple of good old boys."

"Wait a minute," James said. "I think you're getting the wrong idea. I didn't mean anything by the spirits comment. I was just trying to be sensitive to your culture. I wouldn't want you getting involved in nothing that made you regret it later. I want to go on record with that."

"I'll keep it as record," Caleb said. "And that goes for me too. A pet cemetery is a weird and spooky thing to most people. You all don't seem to mind, but I think most would."

"We're not most then, are we?" Daniel said.

"I'm getting to know that," Caleb said.

They were at a standoff then. Russ didn't know where to go from here. He knew that this was the precise moment for which Daniel and Teresa had asked him to come. The only thought that was in Russ's head was about the size of Caleb Moyer. In one way, the droopy jowls and furrowed brow, he looked like a pet himself, a bulldog of some sort. Russ wondered how big a hole would have to be dug to put him inside a cemetery in the backyard. Teresa and Dan couldn't know what he was thinking, but if they could they would have known then why he and his morbid sentiments were not a good fit for their intentions.

There was nothing else to do except come right out with it. "There's no building code or clause about mortality," Russ said.

"I beg your pardon," James said.

"You told Dan and Teresa last time that they couldn't purchase this land because of some 'mortality violation.' There's no such thing."

"And how would you know that for sure?" James asked.

"I searched the whole internet, far and wide. I looked at every website that had to do with the county municipalities or construction commission."

James chuckled. "Well, that must have taken you a long time," he said.

"A whole evening," Russ said.

"Did you happen upon a site called Wellton County Planning.org?" James asked.

"Of course," Russ said. "Scoured it top to bottom."

Caleb and James both seemed to be trying to hide smiles that were too stubborn to lie still on their lips.

"What?" Russ said. He was feeling a little surly now, starting to gain some brass. There was a pulsing tightness in the base of his neck. He did not like to be laughed at.

James looked at his watch. "Calm down," he said. "We've got another man stopping by. He should have been here by now. He'll help sort this out. Let's not get rowdy."

"Nobody is getting rowdy," Teresa said. "We're calm." Then, as if to draw the assertion out into the world, she pivoted to face Daniel and pressed herself into his body. None of them could see what she was doing, but they could hear her whispering something in Spanish. Daniel's face softened as he put his arm around her back and hugged her close.

James checked his watch again, and Caleb made a movement like he had one too, but there was nothing on his wrist. Russ looked back at the house again. It looked so debilitated with its sagging columns and broken windows. Dan and Teresa were fighting for the chance to inhabit what was nothing more than a marred and melted heap of rubble. It angered Russ to think about how this must have been what much of their lives felt like in this country.

A cop car pulled up and parked in back of James's truck. Russ's knees went slack and his head went heavy then light in a dizzying flop. All of a sudden he could feel the pain in his foot start back up again. When Lang stepped out of the car and slammed the door, Russ's nerves vibrated with it. He felt like running. His heart drummed. As he approached with his jangling keys and cuffs and his thudding nightstick all kinds of alarm bells went off inside Russ.

"There he is," said Caleb. He spat a last hunk of tobacco onto the grass. "Officer Lang." He stepped forward to greet him and they shook not only hands but next arms and elbows in a double embrace of camaraderie.

"Morning," Lang said. He tipped his cap to James then nodded in the direction of the others. "James, Daniel, Teresa." His eyes stopped and settled on Russ. Russ dropped his chin to his chest. "Mr. Cooper?" Lang said. "What are you doing here?"

Russ wanted to respond, was worried he might have been doing so involuntarily, but no sound came out.

"We met him a few days ago," Teresa said. She left Daniel and walked over to Russ where she rested a hand on the center of his back. Russ flinched. He whipped his back free of her reach.

"Sorry," Russ said. He took a deep breath, and then the breaths kept coming. He'd seen old movies where someone had to breathe into a brown paper bag, and he felt now like that would be helpful for him.

"You okay?" Lang asked. He moved over beside Russ and peered up at his face. "You don't look so good. You're a little bluish in the gills."

All of the jolting images came rushing back to Russ. The sound of the gunshot and his scrambling inside the tub. The body flat in the alley. His queasy conversation with Lang the next morning. He'd been able to keep them at bay recently, but they were always there smoldering, waiting to be re-ignited.

"He'll be fine," Daniel said. Now Daniel came over and stood next to Russ. He too had an impulse to touch him, but as he raised his hand Teresa caught it and gently collapsed it back down at his side.

"I'm just…" Russ said. "I haven't seen Wesley… Um, Officer Lang since…"

"Oh, I see," Lang said, straightening up. He took a step back and sighed. "He's on edge."

"No," Russ said. "Maybe a little. I'm still shook up, I guess."

"What's going on?" Caleb said. He looked genuinely concerned, but not for Russ. It was unclear exactly what he was worked up about.

"You all remember the Baxter case?" Lang said.

"No!" Russ shouted. He hadn't tried to shout, but it came out that way. All of the coiled-up emotions came firing out of him, betraying him now. "I don't want to talk about that. Please!"

"Whoa," Lang said. "All right. All right, now take it easy."

"That's what I've been telling them," Caleb said. "Calm down."

"Why is he here?" Lang asked.

"What Baxter case?" James said.

"No!" Russ said. "I'm here because..." He took one last exhale of breath, then placed his hand on Teresa's shoulder to hoist himself back up. He nodded at Daniel who at that moment had his mouth open ready to speak. He put his hand up to halt Daniel. "I'm here because there is no bullshit code violation about..." he straightened up completely now on his own volition. "There is no mortality violation."

"Okay now," James said. "Let's everyone cool out. This is why I had Officer Lang come by this morning." He turned to Lang and gestured something with his hand. He made a circular motion, beckoning like he wanted Lang to finish his thought for him. "About, you know. What I told you about last night. You checked it?"

Lang cleared his throat and wiped his mouth with the back of his sleeve. This was what he'd come for. "I read it this morning. According to appendix three in the model ordinances, a building may not be sold or bought within thirty days of a death in the home or until an investigation has been finalized."

"What?" Russ said. "No. No, that was not there before. I checked."

"When did you check?" James asked.

"Three nights ago. I checked."

"Maybe look again," James said. His eyes moved rapidly, first up and to the right, then down at the ground.

Daniel's mouth popped open and stayed agape. "You mean to tell me... You added it in."

"I don't know about that," Lang said. "Just hold on."

"It wasn't there before," Russ said. James still wasn't looking anyone in the eyes.

"It was there when I looked," Lang said. "It's there now. I don't know about two or three or four days ago, but it's inconsequential to our little disagreement here."

Caleb still couldn't hold back or defeat the smug little grin that stretched the corners of his face. Maybe he'd stopped trying now that Lang was there. "They won't believe us anyway."

"Us?" Russ said, darting a look at Caleb.

"The guys have told you," Caleb said, "what we've known about all along. Maybe you missed it before." He shrugged his shoulders, licked his lips. He sort of pressed forward, almost bumping chests with Russ.

If Russ really was Richie, this would be the time where he would slug Caleb right between the eyes. In order to fend off the instinct, he stuck a knuckle in his mouth and sucked on it.

"This isn't fair," Daniel said, stepping back from Caleb.

"That isn't right," said Teresa, and it was making it so much worse now that their tones had changed from anger to sadness. The wind billowed her huge poncho, and she cradled her arms across her stomach to keep it down.

"It doesn't make any sense!" said Russ. He was able to catch James's gaze and freeze it there. "James. James, come on. You know this isn't right."

"Now, James is only doing his job," Lang said. "Ease off. The way it stands, it's not worth fighting over anyway because there's another code, too. There's a second one that's in play."

"No way," Russ said. "There was nothing there about fires or death of any kind."

"This is ridiculous," Teresa said, some of the old fury bubbling up again. Daniel stood behind her now, slumped and silent.

"What is it now?" Russ said. "I can't wait for this. What could it possibly be?"

"If you would let the gentleman speak," Caleb said.

"Ha!" Teresa said. "Gentleman?" She turned to Daniel and grabbed his hand. She squeezed all of her frustration into his fingers. "Pinche puto," she grumbled under her breath.

"Model 4.6!" Lang hollered, trying to drown out Teresa's voice. "It's right there in black and white. Transfer of Development Rights Ordinance (TDR)." He lowered his voice, conscious of the way his authority was being undermined by his timbre. He cleared his throat. "A new property may not be built on a patch of land where ashes have contaminated the soil. I'm paraphrasing, but you get the idea. Nobody has done a full test on the quality of the soil since the fire's ashes have been mixed into the earth surrounding the area. The ground may not even be fit to… well, it's not structurally sound. Did I say that right, James?"

"Yes, you summed it up," James said. "There's a lot of other jargon and technical language that goes into it. Things like potassium, nitrogen, sulfur…"

"That is a load of horse shit, and you know it," Russ said.

"You are out of line," Lang said. "I suggest you watch your words."

"I'm upset," Russ said.

"That is crystal clear," Lang said. "Why are you so wrapped up in this?"

"I'm in it now," Russ said. "The Flores's needed my help, and I'm involved…" He was starting to sweat. His mouth felt dry and sticky. He shouldn't have worn two sweaters. He used one of the sleeves to dab some perspiration away from his forehead.

"Are you sure that's the only thing bothering you?" Lang said.

"Yes!" Russ said.

"You're certain. Nothing else weighing on your conscience?"

"What do you mean?" Russ said. The sweat was coming faster than he could wipe it away.

"You don't look good," Lang said. With every word he took one step closer to Russ until he was standing about two inches from his feet.

Russ had had enough of folks crowding his space, making veiled physical threats. "I don't feel well!" he shouted, moving Lang off a few paces.

"What is going on?" Teresa said. "Why don't you leave him alone?"

"Why are you all so close all of a sudden?" Lang said. "You couldn't have known each other more than a week."

"Give him some space," Daniel said. "He doesn't feel well."

"Come to think of it," Lang said. "When did you all buzz into town exactly?" He switched his glare on Teresa and Daniel.

"We've been here over two weeks, why?" Daniel said.

"So you were around for the murder," Lang said.

"Murder?" Teresa said. "What are you talking about?"

"Oh, you didn't hear?" Lang said. "How could you not have heard? I thought you and Russ were buddies. I thought you were close. You didn't tell them, Russ?"

Russ shook his head. He was trying not to throw up.

"What is going on?" Daniel said.

"What is he talking about?" said Teresa.

"Nothing," Russ said. "It doesn't involve them. They don't need to be burdened with all that."

"Actually, I'm not sure that's accurate," Lang said. "Where are you guys staying?"

"We've been at the Windsor Motel over on Grant Street the whole time," Daniel said.

"The whole time, huh? That's not too far away," Lang said. "Maybe three, four blocks at the most. And you didn't know anything about the shooting?" Lang moved away from Russ, edged his way closer in the Flores' direction. "You didn't hear a gunshot? Any yelling?" He put his hand on his hip, rested it just above the handle of his Glock. "We haven't talked to your family yet."

"Don't answer that," Russ said.

"We've got nothing to hide," Daniel said.

"You wouldn't mind coming down to the station and giving a sworn statement then?"

"Don't go," Russ said. "You don't have to do that."

"We could do that," Daniel said. Teresa grabbed his hand and bore down.

"Good," Lang said.

"No!" Russ said. "Let's leave," Russ said.

"You're free to go if you think that's best." He put his hands up in the air and twisted from side to side. "I'm not forcing or browbeating anyone."

"Let's get out of here," Russ said. He dabbed his face dry. His nose was running, and he mopped it off with his sleeve. His sweater was wet with gross fluids from all kinds of pores.

Daniel and Teresa slowly walked over to Russ, careful to keep their eyes on Lang and the other men. They'd walked like this before, Russ could tell, cautious not to move in any way that could be deemed threatening or erratic. They walked away down the sidewalk together, Russ in the middle and the Flores's flanking him. Every two or three strides, Daniel and Teresa would peer over their shoulders. Teresa's hand was shaking. She put it in her pocket and kept going.

"You're limping," Daniel said.

"It's okay," Russ said. "I'm fine." It occurred to Russ that this was the final piece, that now, with the bum ankle, he'd gone full method into his role as Richie, though it didn't feel like he was pulling it off.

"You would tell us if there was something bad," Daniel said.

"Yes, I would tell you. You don't have to ask."

"That wasn't a question," Daniel said.

When they were a half a block away, Russ peered over his own moist and heated shoulder. What he saw were three small men clustered together on the curb, two of them in stature and one in mindset only. He hadn't noticed before how similar James and Lang looked. They could have been twins, two diminutive boys born to the same dwarf parents. And now they were no doubt parents themselves, guarding their little ones against unseen or unknown dangers - murderers, arsons, outsiders and the well-educated. There would be no more fires on their watch. But the soil was already tainted. They said it themselves. In case there weren't enough already, they had concocted their own fears that could not be explained away. The three of them stood there feeling the power they had, their collective barricade designed to stop imaginary intruders from invading their hypothetical, disfigured fortress.

"This isn't over," Daniel said.

"No," said Russ. "There is always more."

"Shhhh, not now," Teresa said. She let her head go limp against Russ's shoulder and rested it there. "You did a good job," she said.

He was glad that she thought so. He had done his best. The sun was higher in the sky now and the rays came seeping through the leafless autumn trees. The branches swayed in the breeze. His sweat had turned chilly against his skin. There was already the promise of a cold and windy sundown later on. Far away now, barely visible in the distance, were the free, haphazard items on the sidewalk, a strange mound of leftovers from a stranger's personal collection. Russ thought for a split second that his eye caught something sparkly in the mix, a set of silverware or a diamond perhaps. But then the flicker was gone, and Russ knew it was only the oily reflection from the rain puddle next to the box. It didn't seem like this should be the way things ended for those lonesome possessions. It seemed like a disrespectful sendoff, like a funeral without any mourners. Lots of things were starting to feel that way to Russ. The world was trying to tell him that there were realizations he needed to make friends with. Nothing would be over in any recognizable way again. After the last few weeks, he knew, nothing would ever end in any clear-eyed or predictable pattern again.

7

Richie asked Russ if Thursday night he could swing by and take him to run some errands after dinner. This was not a common request, but Russ agreed even though he was concerned that this could turn into another long night of whiskey drinking and driving aimless circles around the grounds of Valley View again. The truth was, Russ had nothing better to do. He hadn't really left his house in a week other than to throw out his trash or step outside for a smoke break. Now and then the occasional slamming of the dumpster lid in the back alley would send him into a spasm of flashback terror, and that got his heart pumping, but other than that his life had become one long stagnant stretch. It was starting to get pitiful. All he did was go to work, come home, watch old reruns of Bob's Burgers and get stoned. He was on a run of getting stoned now, not just high. A few days ago there was a scene on Bob's Burgers where the Belcher's teacher, Coach Blevins, thought that he'd made friends with some of his students, but they were all making fun of him behind his back. One of the kids said, "He talks to himself all the time, and the weirdest thing is that I don't even think he realizes he's doing it. I think he thinks all those words are only playing out inside his own head." And then there's this whole montage of Coach Blevins walking around the basketball court or going through the lunchline in the cafeteria while talking out loud about his bad date the night before or his pet corgi's unhealthy diet or his fears about students discovering his obsession with cross-dressing as Blanche Devereaux from the 19080s sitcom Golden Girls. Russ laughed at first, but then spent the next forty-five minutes lost in a daze of troubling questions about his own self-talking habits. A couple times in the past few weeks he'd caught himself talking through a difficult conversation on the toilet when nobody else was around or acting out a particularly delicate interaction as a rehearsal to the pending encounter. Had he been doing this for a long time? How many people had noticed and not said anything? Did he do this often? Was this why he hadn't made any new friends in the last few years? Were people talking about him? These paranoid thoughts swirled around inside his fried brain until he almost picked up the phone and called Molly. She'd tell him the truth. She'd know if he'd been embarrassing himself like Coach Blevins during the time they were sleeping together, and she'd let him know straight. She'd do that for him. He had every intention of picking up the phone and making the call, but the next thing he knew he was waking up on the couch with a bag of Cheetos in his lap and one hand down his sweatpants. The phone was on the floor and the log showed that he hadn't made a single outgoing call in almost six days. He didn't know whether to celebrate or cry, but he was relieved. Maybe that was why Richie had called and invited him Thursday. Richie had a way of picking up on these things. He was like a depression bloodhound, probably because he knew the familiar scent as well or better than just about anyone else in town.

Richie said seven o'clock, but Russ was so bored and tired of watching TV, that he left his apartment at six-thirty. He knew that it only took about twelve minutes to drive to Richie's house, but if he was subjected to one more delirious commercial about car insurance or took one more hit off of his bubbler, he was certain he'd either pass out or hang himself from the shower rod with the only necktie he owned.

The streets of Wellton on Thursday nights looked and felt about the same as the rooms of his apartment back home, dead silent, vacant and dimly ominous. The only car he saw during the entire trip was a rattling Oldsmobile with one headlight out and a badly bent radio antenna. The angle at which it was bent made Russ think that somebody would have had to attack it with malicious intent. At the light, Russ pulled up beside the battered vehicle to make a right turn. He liked picturing the ancient and waify man inside with enemies waiting around every corner to enact their vengeance. This geezer, Russ thought, had the grizzled and gnarly face of a man who had done some things in life that he needed to pay for. Or maybe he was just too high for his own good again. It was getting hard to tell.

When Russ arrived at Richie's he was surprised to find just about every light off in the entire house. To the casual observer, it looked as though nobody was home at all. Even the porch light, the lone yellow bulb above the front door that stayed on night and day was out. All that was visible up on the shadowy porch was the outline of a wobbly folding chair and a large stone ashtray overflowing with soggy cigarette butts and crumpled Marlboro packs. Richie had told Russ once that his mom, Ashley Hess, liked to watch scary movies with all the lights off inside. Psychological thrillers were her favorite. Richie's job was to make snacks and sit near enough to her on the couch so that if she needed something to grab onto in her fright his arm would be within reach. He'd showed Russ a bruise on his forearm a few weeks ago that had resulted from a particularly spooky showing of a thriller called *A Quiet Place*. There was something about that image, those small acts of devotion, that drew Russ out of his car and compelled him to creep around the house and peek inside. It was a big and assertive structure, the kind that made one feel as though they were embarking on an intrepid journey just to reach the other side. Along the property line, several towering oak trees crackled and swayed in the breeze. They threw jagged, flickering patterns against the green siding as Russ made his way toward the faint light in back.

Russ approached the glowing window with great care. This was the window, he knew, that faced straight into the kitchen and then through that room into the family room with the sofa and television, the space where Richie and his mom shared all their most private moments together. It was a sort of sacred place and Russ moved upon it with that reverence in mind. He wiggled behind a juniper bush and peered through the glass. What he found made him question his brazen trespassing, but he could not look away. Richie was locked in a sort of stooped and strenuous embrace with Ashley in the middle of the family room. He had his arms wedged under her armpits as she tilted all of her weight against his wide sternum. His body absorbed the load knees first, folding slightly before bracing into a sturdy column. Her face was the one angled toward Russ's at the window. It looked tired and old. Russ didn't know how old she actually was, but it didn't matter. Whatever age her body was supposed to be, her face was too old for it. On the coffee table behind the wheelchair Russ could see an open bottle of pills, a rumpled sweatshirt and a white plate smeared with melted orange cheese. The way Richie cradled Ashley and rocked her into place on the seat's vinyl cushion was the most gentle maneuver Russ had ever seen him perform. How could that physique, the broad and burly back that Russ now witnessed nestle a frail mother into place, be the same one that not three months ago took a baseball bat across it in the parking lot outside Brogan's Tap? They both took deep sighs now as Richie adjusted Ashley's heels onto the footplates and brushed the silvered hair out of her eyes.

The story behind why Richie was hit with a bat is a difficult one to tell. In its simplist form, it is a tale of a man who couldn't keep his mouth closed, but there is more to it than that. It started when Richie felt the urge to concern himself over the way Calvin Yeager was treating the reputation of his little sister.

Now Richie got behind the wheelchair and began rolling it around the chairs in the kitchen. The chairs were all clustered together, tangled at the legs, and Richie had to stop and shove them out of the way.

That night at Brogans, Calvin, as Richie saw it, was sitting idly by while his buddies said blasphemous things about his kid sister. A few of them more than insinuated that she spread her legs for every other guy in town. This happened to be one of those occasions, which one could never predict, when Richie felt like making it his business to stand up for the honor of a random person. They hardly knew Calvin's sister, Heidi. The only thing Russ knew about her was that she liked to hang out at college parties when she was only fifteen or sixteen. She'd show up on Wellton's campus with her tight and high-waisted jeans on and her long silk hair that came down almost to the waistband of those same denim huggers. A couple of times he'd seen her around town, hitching rides in the back of pickup trucks, that streaming brown hair flapping in the breeze, and always with the type of lawless guys who shouldn't be trusted with that kind of cargo. He didn't know how much Richie knew, but it couldn't have been much more than that. He should have been able to leave the conversation alone. But he just couldn't do it. He just couldn't sit there listening anymore as the rednecks up at the bar called Heidi a slut and a whore. And it wasn't even them he was after but her brother, Calvin. Instead of looking at the guys doing the name-calling, Richie kept his eyes on Calvin, wondering when he was going to step in and do something to defend the honor of his sister. The longer it went on the more riled Richie got. After the brutes went all in, saying that Heidi had given blowjobs to the entire Hershey Bears hockey team, and Calvin himself started laughing along, Richie stood up and came for him. He'd been over at the pool table earlier, and for whatever reason he still had his stick. He held the pole in one hand and his beer in the other. In Russ's mind he can still hear the clacking of balls over on the pool table in the background. Even sitting down, Calvin's bald and wrinkled head was almost as high as Richie's shoulder standing up. He was not the hearty muscular type of fat like Richie but more rotund and beefy. Calvin was an ugly man, the kind that made you wonder how two siblings could possibly be from the same parents. Russ remembers him coming in tight to Calvin at the bar, nuzzling in so close that Russ was sure he was going to whisper in his ear, but he didn't. He spoke loud enough for everyone to hear. Right into his ear he said, "If you don't think somebody calling your little sister a fuck toy is grounds for throwing a punch, I feel very safe telling you to your face that you are a cowardly piece of shit." Richie slammed his empty beer glass down on the bar and left to use the bathroom. He took the pool stick with him just in case. Either Calvin was too shocked or too scared to respond right away. He just sat there and drained his beer. Russ watched him gulp it down. When he was finished he slapped some bills on the table and tottered up from his stool. He was a clumsy and bloated looking mess, but he was thick and tall. There seemed to be no neck in between his chin and chest, like a Humpty Dumpty doll only drunk and frown-faced.

When Richie came back from the john he was pissed to find that Calvin was gone.

Ashley pulled the blanket from the back of her chair and draped it over her legs. Richie wheeled her up against the kitchen table and locked the wheels. As Richie moved to leave her side, she reached over her shoulder and clasped his hand in hers. They stayed like that for a few seconds, quiet and smiling together in their own pocket of solitude, and then Richie moved off to find some food in the refrigerator. The wallpaper must have been leftover from the 1970s, peeling yellow patterns of wheat and barley blended with forty years of grease stains. Russ could imagine Richie and Ashley sitting around smoking and staring at that paper, knowing they had neither the funds to replace it nor the energy to repair something that was already past the point of saving. Maybe it was Richie's dad who had splashed the oil, a careless steak maker or bacon lover. It was this thought that made Russ take a step back and pause. The sight of Richie unwrapping cellophane from a crusty pot and pulling down chipped dishware from the cabinets while his mom looked on in admiration was too much to bear. He had intruded upon something too intimate to witness in secret. It was a violation in the worst possible way. Russ slid back from the window and shuffled his way out from behind the shrub. His steps were slow and cautious at first but turned faster as he neared the car, each stride bringing a larger sense of regret and shame.

Two or three hours later, after last call at Brogans, when Russ and Richie had gone swaying out to their car, Calvin Yeager popped out from behind a dumpster and hit Richie as hard as he could with a Louisville Slugger. Before they knew what happened Calvin took flight, huffing and chugging as he held his drooping jeans up with one chubby hand and swatted tree branches out of his way with the other.

It was a full fifteen minutes later when Richie finally came out of the house. Russ could hear him getting closer, coughing and snorting, blowing his nose on the sleeve of his sweatshirt. As he opened the door he let out a monster belch.

"Whoa!" he said, "that was a dinger."

"You're fucking disgusting," Russ said.

"Deal with it," Richie said.

"Hey, I'm the one doing you a favor."

"Yep."

"Yep?"

"Yep."

"You've got nothing else to say for yourself?" Russ asked.

"Nope," Richie said.

Russ shook his head. He started the car and pulled out onto the road.

"Where are we going?" Russ asked.

"Ebberly," Richie said.

"Ebberly?" Russ said.

"Dude," Richie said, "is there a fucking echo in here?" He whipped his head around, checking the backseat for anything that might cause unexplained reverberation.

Russ started to say something mean but stopped. He was going to say that Ebberly was at least ten miles away, and he didn't sign up for this shit.

"Sorry I was late," Richie said. "Mom's having a bad one tonight. I think I might have to take her back to therapy again in the morning."

Russ nodded. He sucked his teeth. "It's all right," he said. "Ebberly is cool. I hear it's beautiful this time of year." Richie laughed hard. His whole body came thrusting forward and he slapped the dashboard. It was rare to get a laugh like this out of him, and it felt good. "Can we at least stop at Hardees afterward?"

"Oh, shit yeah," Richie said. "We have to!"

They both laughed until they were crying, and Richie had to get his handkerchief out of his pocket and dry his eyes. Hardees was only funny because they used to go to the one in Ebberly all the time back in high school. They'd get high and drunk, way too tipsy to drive, and then drive out to Ebberly for some Hardees because it was the only fast food place with a dining room that stayed open twenty-four hours. They always thought it was hilarious to have a Hardees open around the clock. If you were there between about eleven and one in the morning, you'd see just about every type of tweaker or pervert or nut job you'd ever want to meet. They thought it was funny for a long time until they realized that they were starting to become part of the crowd themselves, and once that realization set in it took hold pretty fast. Neither one of them had been back since. They hadn't really talked about it at the time and nobody had even mentioned it in the past five or six years, which was why Russ's call-back made them crack-up so much.

When Russ and Richie were growing up Ebberly seemed like a big city. It had record shops and bookstores and cafes that seemed more stylish and sophisticated than the ones Wellton had to offer. It also seemed edgier and faster like a big city. Their downtown was similar to Wellton's in that it also had charm and old fashioned appeal, but on their sidewalks you'd be more likely to find Black families or Asian ones, business men carrying briefcases or women in high heels bustling to their jobs as lawyers or bankers. There was more industry in Ebberly which also meant more movement and vibrancy. It also meant more divides between rich and poor which also meant more crime and friction. It was a small big city, and like others cut from that mold it had grit and seduction in the form of strip clubs and a state prison. And like other similar cities around the country, a reckoning had descended upon it in the past decade or two. Instead of family run places like grocery stores or local dress shops there were humongous WalMarts and outlet malls. The change was slow but total and profound, so that by the time people were upset or ready to fight, the only places left were abandoned warehouses and shuttered storefronts covered in dust. There'd been a bit of a resurgence in the last few years, including a renovated marketplace with farmstand produce and added parkland with lots of greenery, but it was not enough to keep the real entrepreneurs in town.

What Richie and Russ saw as they drove up Lehman Street toward downtown were the flunkies left behind by the caucasian migration. They reached an intersection where on the right side a homeless man was sleeping in the doorway of a vacant shoe store, and on the left side, spilling more out into the line of traffic with every manic second, a pair of vagrants without many teeth arguing in furious tones and gestures. As the fight reached the center lane Russ had to honk the horn to get them to move. It must have been a lovers' quarrel because as they scurried back onto the curb the man tried kissing the woman and she struck him across the face with a closed fist.

"Ooooooooo, shiiiiiiiiiiit!" Russ hissed.

"Ouch!" Richie said. "Damn! That looked painful."

The car was still coasting along, but Russ was not looking at the road. He was too captivated by the altercation. It had moved onto stage two, a streak of whirling bodies more akin to a dance than a dispute. Each of them had ahold of the other's shirt collar and they twirled round and round the pavement, bobbing and arching to some unheard waltz. It was hypnotizing. The woman was about to lose the shirt right up over her head. The only thing keeping the man from tearing it clean off was the woman's two starchy pigtails sticking straight out on both sides of her head like frizzy handlebars. "Oh my God!" Russ said.

"Yo!" Richie shouted. "Watch out. Turn. Turn. Right here. Right!"

Russ pumped the brakes and spun the wheel to the right. It could have been worse had he been going over fifteen miles per hour, but he hadn't so all that happened was he clipped the low curb with one tire and came to a jolting stop behind a line of other parked cars. The street was narrow and claustrophobic. It must have been a one way street because there was no way two cars could fit down going opposite directions. Russ didn't think he'd ever been on this street before. It was so tiny. Was it a street or an alleyway? What caught the eye were mostly back gates and garages that led to small row homes fronting the larger street on the other side. Russ looked around for a street sign but couldn't find any.

"There," Richie said, pointing a few houses down on the left. "You can park here. This is fine. It's just up ahead."

Russ squinted into the distance but couldn't make anything out. Whatever this lane or road was it wasn't lit by any street lamps or floodlights.

"I swear to God, if you're taking me to meet with some meth dealer, I'm leaving your ass right here on the side of the road," Russ said.

"Jesus, what do you take me for?" Richie said. He opened his door and stepped out onto the asphalt. Russ followed. He stepped outside and closed the door, but he kept his fingers on the handle. "It's heroine night," Richie said. Russ pulled the door open and was halfway back inside before Richie called him back out again. "Oh come on," he said. "Relax. It's nothing like that."

"Nothing like heroine?" Russ said.

Richie put his hands in the pockets of his soiled Adidas jacket and spit a loogie onto the ground. "Well, it will make you feel good, but not in the same way. Similar I guess, but not really." He started walking up the street. He crossed over to the other side and continued up the sidewalk.

Russ was still standing outside the car with his fingers on the door handle. He wasn't ready to make up his mind yet, but as Richie got farther away, and his figure began to disappear in the darkness, Russ got spooked. He thought he heard a door slam or maybe a car backfire. Whatever it was, he wasn't about to stick around and find out. He closed the door and sprinted after Richie. "Hey!" he said. "Wait up!"

Russ caught up to him just as he was about to enter onto a property that looked like a regular private residence. It was a squat white house with a black door and a set of crumbling stairs bracketed by a dingy black railing. The door looked like it had been clawed into by a savage dog or gashed open by the blade of a knife. Above it hung one dim bulb and below that a wooden sign that said "Hype Video" in runny blue paint. There were a few faded movie posters and a couple of video game advertisements pasted in the window. One movie was called "Sins of Desire." It featured a woman dressed in a slinky negligee with a scoop of shimmering cleavage showing. She was hugging herself and she had her mouth parted open with her head flung back. It would have been sexy except the woman looked like she was at least fifty, and it must have been made in the 1990s, so whoever it was had to be at least sixty or seventy by now. There was an ad for a video game called "Night Trap" that he had never heard of before. There was a woman on the cover who looked horrified. She was also dressed in some scanty nightgown, but it was a cartoon drawing and the masked burglar in the background looked so silly that it was hard to take seriously. That didn't make the whole scene less disturbing, though. Why would there be a video game about scaring women in their underwear? For a second Russ thought it might actually be a movie of some kind, but right there on the bottom of of the poster was the Sega logo and a tagline that read, "Play two and a half hours of real video!" Wait, Russ thought. It's real or it's a game? Russ kept reading it over and over. It didn't make sense.

Richie grabbed the door knob and Russ clamped his hand around Richie's wrist.

"Dude," Richie said. "You are freaking out."

"What is this place?" Russ asked.

"It's a video store, dude."

"Yeah, but… a video store? Like a Blockbuster?"

"You could say that, I guess. I mean it's not a franchise or anything."

"Clearly!" Russ said.

Richie took his hand off the knob. He snatched his wrist back and put both hands on Russ's shoulders. He gave them a little shake. "Look, man. Pull yourself together. It's a video store. Calm down. Breathe, dude. Jesus."

"Yeah, but what are we doing here? I didn't even know places like this existed anymore."

"I'm looking for a specific type of video," Richie said.

"Can't you find it online?" Russ asked.

Richie shook his head.

"This place is weird," Russ said. "It's creepy."

"No shit," Richie said. "But it's just a place like any other, man. It's a place of business. It does specialty retail, which is super rare these days. You might actually dig it."

"You're not looking for like some black market rape fantasy shit are you?"

"All right," Richie said, "now you're just hurting my feelings." He raised his hands in frustration, let them slap down against his thighs.

"I'm sorry," Russ said.

"I have feelings, you know?"

"I know."

"That was over the line."

"Yeah," Russ said.

"Not cool," Richie said.

"Yeah okay," Russ said. "I said I'm sorry."

"Okay, I'm gonna go inside now. I'm gonna do what I came to do. I'll tell you all about it if you come along or you can wait outside here on the stoop listening to crickets and picking your nose or whatever. I don't care. But I really need to do this tonight."

Richie heaved open the door and pushed inside. The hinges seemed to be rusted over so that it took all of Richie's force to pry the thing open. Russ took one step toward the door and then one back toward the sidewalk. He heard the crickets Richie talked about. There must have been a thousand of them hiding somewhere, all joining together. They seemed to get louder and closer with every chirp. He would never see them coming in this darkness. If they wanted to swarm him he wouldn't notice until they were all on top of him. The posters were making him nervous. The frightened, naked women wouldn't stop staring at him. If he ran their eyes would just follow him. The only way to escape their unsettling gaze was to go inside. He ran at the door and flung it open. As he plowed inside, before the door could come springing back, he found himself mashed against Richie's massive chest. Richie wrapped his arms around him and squeezed.

"Shhh," he said. "Shhhhh. There, there. Chill, bro."

"What the?" Russ said, nose pressed deep into the folds of his Adidas jacket. "What are you doing?"

Richie spoke in a steady, hushed voice. "I was just about to go back out and get you. I wasn't going to let you stranded out there. I know you've been feeling on edge lately. You're going through some things, and I was thinking that it wasn't the right call to just leave you standing out there all alone. Okay?"

Russ was suffocating. There was something in his mouth from the jacket, a wad of dog fur maybe or a mesh of loose thread. He tried spitting it out. "Dude, your coat smells like Corn Nuts! It's a landfill in here. Let me out!" Russ pushed back against Richie's chest at the same time Richie released him. Russ staggered back, tripping and cracking his back on a wooden shelf. A few thin boxes bounced off the wall and clattered to the floor. Russ stooped to pick them up. "Sorry!" he said to no one in particular. "Sorry!"

The whole time he was apologizing he was looking around the room for anyone who may have been offended by the spectacle. As he stood and placed the DVDs back on the shelf, he located what must have been the clerk up at the front of the store. He was standing behind a high counter with a big glass showcase underneath. It was filled with movie candy - Milk Duds, Whoppers, JujyFruits. Over his shoulder was the window that was plastered with all of the freaky posters and advertisements. He was looking at something on his cell phone, stuck in a hazy, neverending thumb-scroll. The blank and drugged look on his face made it clear that he was not concerned about a few dropped DVD cases. His mouth was dangling open in a way that reminded Russ of what his dad used to say about catching flies if you weren't careful. He wore a striped red and yellow shirt that was trying to stretch for his waist but only had strength enough to reach the top of his belly button.

"What up, Ronald?" Richie said. He raised a fist in the guy's direction, flashed a peace sign.

"Hey," Ronald said. He kept his head down, continued on with his scrolling and drooling. Above his head a grainy, flickering TV screen played some kind of gangster movie. *Reservoir Dogs* maybe or *Pulp Fiction*? Something with a bunch of guys dressed in suits and waving guns around.

"Come on," Richie said. He motioned for Russ to get behind him and keep up.

Richie led him along a wood-paneled wall with jagged wooden shelves that stretched from the very base of the floor to the very edge of the ceiling. It was all made of the same cheap and craggy wood; rife with stray splinters and rugged static. There seemed to be no logic behind the organization. Comedy movies were housed next to crime dramas. Different eras were mixed together. The *Terminator* series was lined up alongside kids movies like *Toy Story.* A Jeff Foxworthy stand-up special was two boxes down from *Waterworld.* Everything was from the 90s. The oddest thing was the cramped design of the shelving units. A man would need a yardstick and his tiptoes to reach the titles on the top shelf, and somebody would have to lie flat on their stomach to view the films on the bottom shelf. And nobody would want to be down on the floor. It was covered in the kind of ripped and stained carpet that nobody would want to lie down on. At first Russ thought it was beige with a little brown woven in for texture, but then he realized the brown parts were trails of cookie crumbs or dried cola that were never washed out.

"So, all right," Richie said. "Here's what I'm doing." He was moving fast, putting more distance between them, and Russ had to jog just so he didn't lose him. He was talking fast, too. It was hard to make out what he was saying because he wasn't turning his head when he spoke so all of his words were aimed at the walls. "My uncle, Martin, he has problems. I mean, it's not his fault. Well, sort of..." He was speaking loudly, but it was only the three of them in the whole place, and he guessed Richie wasn't too concerned about Ronald. "He has lung cancer, so you know? There's a lot that goes into it. Anyway, he's probably only got about three months left." Richie stopped moving.

"Whoa!" Russ said. He had to put his hands up to keep from slamming into Richie again.

Right in front of Richie was one of those retro beaded curtains that click together when someone pushes through them. This one was a solid brown color, but Russ had seen some before that were decorated with silly paintings like a smiling Budha or the Mona Lisa. Richie put one palm on the middle strands and hovered there. There was a pink neon sign on one of the wood panels beside it that read: "Adults Only."

"I know what you're thinking," Richie said. "Not all of my family is dying or disabled. I've got a healthy aunt, a few cousins. I have some very healthy grandparents actually. Three out of the four of them are still living and two of them are almost eighty!"

"I didn't say anything," Russ said.

"Well, just in case you were thinking it," Richie said. He parted the beads open. They clacked together as he stepped through and Russ turned to see it flutter shut behind them. "Anyway, he likes porn." He was so candid, so unbridled. Russ knew that nobody was listening, but still it seemed inappropriate somehow. Russ could never talk like that in public. He was too private, too modest. His parents had made him that way. If he ever so much as saw either one of them with their shirts off he couldn't recall. He still blushed at the sight of any bare skin below the neckline. "But he's very particular. That's why we're here."

It was a small cube of a room, like a storage locker, only instead of old family pictures or antiques it was filled with empty VHS boxes covered in bare-skinned nymphs clutching at each other's breasts and moaning into a camera. Russ's face went hot and flush. He turned red all over. He never would have guessed how squeamish he'd be around all of this lewdness.

"They only have VHS," Russ said.

"The only people left who still go to actual video stores are old people who haven't upgraded their technology since like 1997," Richie said. Something caught his eye. He walked over to the back corner and crouched down to have a closer look.

"Let me get this straight," Russ said. "Your sick uncle asks you to buy him porn because he's dying, but he still needs to get off, and he doesn't have the internet?"

"He doesn't necessarily ask me to do anything." Richie pulled a box off the shelf and held it up close to his face. He squinted as he read the description on the back.

Russ stood in the center and scanned the room. Something about the restricted nature of the space, made him feel under surveillance. He couldn't locate any cameras on the walls or ceilings, but that didn't eliminate the sensation of being watched. His forehead started to sweat. If someone were to come in right now and catch him floundering here he would probably scream. He had no frame of reference for this place. In the past, if he had found himself in an area that made him feel uncomfortable, he could avert his eyes, let them settle on something less distressing, but here there was no escape, no refuge. The first box he spotted had a picture on the front of a nude woman with some sort of electrodes hooked to her ears. Hovering over her head was a spaceship trying to beam her up into the sky. Across the top of the box was the title, *Femalien.* Along the bottom the tagline read: "Beyond human desire." Another box featured a woman with bright red lipstick kissing the tongue of a rattlesnake. Next to that was one with a cheeky looking coed bending down to pick up a textbook with her skirt hiked over her waist. Never before had he felt so guilty, so seen. This was what it was like before the advent of home computers, back when other people could still monitor your tastes, mark you as a deviant or weirdo.

Russ didn't know what to do with his eyes in a place like this. There was nowhere to hide, nowhere to look.

"How do you know what you're searching for?" Russ asked.

"Well," Richie said, putting one box back on the shelf and raising to eye another on a higher ledge. "He likes girl-next-door type stuff," he said. "He wants the female lead to be inexperienced but curious, you know? Like, when she does finally decide to go for it, she'll come out of her shell and have all of these unexpected moves. She'll be in control. And he wants the sex to look real and sort of gentle and loving."

It was incredible how casual Richie was being about the conversation. He spoke about cancer and pornography the way some people chatted about a Phillies baseball game.

"I don't think I've ever seen anything like that before," Russ said.

"He calls it softcore/bad ass. But nothing gratuitous or overly explicit. Mostly kissing and petting. Strictly single X." He put another box down and skimmed the shelves closely, running his palm along each glossy surface as he crept down the rows.

"Yeah, but, I mean, is that even a thing?" Russ asked. "Is it even possible to find something like that?"

"Oh, absolutely not," Richie said. "Hell no. But it's the thought that counts, right? It makes him happy." He grabbed down another case. This one had a woman on the cover wearing a skimpy white nightgown with netted stockings. It must have been set in London because Russ could see the Big Ben clock tower in the background. *Embrace of the Vampire* it was called. "Thrill of the hunt, you know."

When Richie turned around with the box in his hand Russ was standing motionless in the middle of the room looking pale. "How long will this take you?" Russ asked.

"Sometimes I get really intense," Richie said. "I go deeeeeeep into the details, but I can see you're uncomfortable, so I'll speed it up. I won't take too long. Why don't you go back out front and browse?" He said. "They've got a ton of old vintage shit, like all of the stuff that people are crazy for, you know, like all those shows and movies everyone is rebooting right now so that they can relive some part of their childhood or whatever. I'm telling you, places like this are going to make a comeback."

It was hard to take him seriously in this space, smiling and winking, holding an empty VHS sleeve with a half-naked Alyssa Milano on the cover. There was no getting away from the gross or disturbing parts of this process. But then there was also the care and generosity that Richie brought to the search. Who else would do something like this for their bedridden uncle? What an awful and selfless act.

"Yeah, I'll wait out front," Russ said. "Good idea."

"Yeah," Richie said. "I won't be much longer."

"Okay," Russ said.

"Cool."

"Cool."

Russ stood there for a minute longer, watching Richie read the back of the Vampire box. He studied each word of it, holding it close to his face, tracing his finger across every sentence.

Back outside the beaded curtain things had changed. There were more people inside now. It gave Russ a little jolt to see them there. Before this time he couldn't picture anyone entering the store, and now that they were here he was having trouble adjusting. In his mind it had been a place that stayed open only for Richie. It remained in business for the sole purpose of Richie fulfilling his uncle's obscure pornography wishes. When his uncle and his eccentric tastes died so would the store.

There were three of them bunched together; three youthful looking boys, seniors in high-school maybe or college freshman, with moppy hair and sagging jeans. They were gathered around the entrance, laughing and pointing at the box that one of the boys held in his hands.

"Same thing we do every night, Pinky," one of them said in a high squeaky voice.

Another one raised his open hand, then snapped it shut like a claw. "Take over the world!" he shouted. "Pinky and the Motherfucking Brain," he said. "Yes!"

They all shook with laughter. One of them snatched the box away from his friend and slid it under his jacket. "This is mine!" he said. "Screw you guys."

"That's cool," the boy said, shrugging. "Whatever. There's a lot more dope shit over here." He turned his attention toward the back of the store and headed off in that direction.

It did seem that there was an endless supply of retro paraphernalia. Richie was right about the reboots and nostalgia. Everywhere Russ looked there was another vintage movie poster or a crate of old Nintendo games. Next to one of the aisles there was a life-size cutout of Jeff Goldblum from Jurassic Park. Russ was starting to realize that all of the items that had been set out in full display were of the same whimsical variety. Russ began thinking that out of all of the playful relics that had been selected for exhibit it was perhaps most telling to note the more profound options that had been left out. He was starting to wonder if there was even a single item in the whole place that either carried serious merit or was representative of any time period past 1999. Even the boys themselves looked like they were from a different era. One of them was wearing a shiny white polo with a wide pointy collar. Another one sported a blousy striped button-down with the top three buttons undone. All of them had much longer hair than was usual for Ebberly locals, which made Russ wonder whether they were visiting from another town. Judging by the one with the lengthy blond ponytail they could have come from someplace really faroff, maybe even California. Russ couldn't think of one boy he'd ever seen from Ebberly with a ponytail before.

The boy moving toward the back of the store, the one with the ponytail, was getting closer to the beaded curtain. Russ felt nervous for Richie. He couldn't bear the idea of someone walking in on him while he was inside doing something so vulnerable. He knew that Richie probably wouldn't care, but it didn't matter. Russ couldn't help but feel anxious on his behalf. Russ followed after the boy. He wasn't sure what he would do if he caught up to him or if the boy tried to walk inside the adult section, but nonetheless he tracked him. The boy was wearing one of those faded and droopy jackets that are found on bargain racks in the rear of of almost all Salvation Armies. It was navy blue and corduroy with button cuffs and white letters on the back. As Russ got closer he could see that it was one of those old FFA jackets, the kind that usually have eagle patches sewn on the back, but this one had words instead. "Wellton County Hunters" it said in white felt lettering. Some of the felt letters were starting to peel loose from their stitching, but that just added even more character and intrigue to its origins. In fact, once Russ read it he couldn't look away. Wellton County Hunters. What kind of group or team could that possibly be representing? What exactly did they hunt and why did they need to advertise? It's not like hunting was a competitive sport, was it? It opened the mind to all sorts of questions. There was something about the effort that went into the making of the garment. What was the story behind its inception? Russ couldn't stop thinking about it. How mysterious. How alluring… He had to ask him about it. He was overcome.

The boy made his move for the beaded curtain, but Russ caught him in time. "Excuse me," Russ said. The boy paused, his arm stretched halfway through the curtain up to his elbow. "Can I ask you a question?"

"Huh," the boy said. His head snapped around and with it the ponytail. The blond tip swung around his shoulder, lashing him across the neck. "What?"

"Can I ask you about your jacket?" The boy's expression changed from one of dismay to one of good humor. He smiled wide, reeled his full arm back outside the curtain.

"Sure," he said. "Ask away." He backed away from the door, put his hands inside the pockets of his jeans.

"Well, I mean," Russ said. "I guess my first question is what is it?"

The boy laughed. He shook his head.

"What?" Russ said.

"Nothing," the boy said. "I get that question all the time."

"Oh," Russ said. "So what do you say?"

"I say I have no idea." He laughed again. He had a very broad and chipper smile, the kind that made you think he'd be easy to joke around with. Russ was reminded again of his fondness for people who were free and generous with their laughter.

The boy's laughter grew in volume until it overtook Russ too, and then they were both laughing. A couple of pals already. "So, why do you have it? I mean, where did you get it?"

"I found it at the thrift shop on 12th Street, and I have it because it's a good conversation starter. Case and point," he said. He withdrew his hand from his pocket and swung it in Russ's direction for a shake.

Russ didn't catch the gesture right away. "What do you think it means?" Russ said. Then, noticing the hand still dangling there, he accepted it, They shook but with no real affirmation or connection attached.

"You're asking the right questions, buddy," the boy said. "I have the same ones. My hope is that one day I'll be walking around and somebody will come up to me and ask me how in the world I was ever able to find such a rare and meaningful jacket. They'll tell me some long story about how their brother or uncle belonged to the society of Wellton County Hunters back in 1991 or something like that. They can tell me all about the meaning and the background. I can't wait to hear it!"

"That would be awesome," Russ said.

"It's going to happen one day," he said. "Instead of questions, somebody's going to have the answers."

"I almost feel like giving you my cell number so you can call me when it happens."

"I have a half dozen numbers saved in my phone right now from people like you."

"You're kidding," Russ said.

"I'm not," the boy said.

"I love it," Russ said.

"Me too. It gives me something to look forward to."

"A hunt of your own."

"Yes!" the boy said. "Exactly!" There was so much glee and excitement in his voice. "Everyone's searching for something."

Russ liked that a whole myth and philosophy had grown out of something so simple as a jacket. He was about to introduce himself and re-shake hands for real this time when Richie came sliding out of the beaded curtain. He had two VHS boxes sandwiched in his right hand, and he was smiling. He didn't even seem to notice the boy with the ponytail standing right in front of him.

"You're not going to believe what I found," Richie said.

"Jackpot!" the boy said.

Without looking at the boy or even acknowledging his presence, he put his hand on Russ's shoulder and steered him toward the checkout counter. "Let's go to Hardees," he said. "My treat."

8

Russ came into the bank on Friday morning feeling baked and plump like an overcooked hot dog from Hardee's all-night menu. His shirt was too tight, which wasn't helping with the discomfort, and his tie hung sideways across the bloated middle. Some ties just wouldn't hang straight no matter what one did. Those needling inconveniences, life's small tangles, were some of Russ's biggest source of aggravation. It was the universe's way of mocking you, letting you know how insignificant you were at every turn. Little things were always the worst, until a big thing came along and then…

"You're late," Wayne said. He was hunched over a sprawl of papers on the front desk. He'd made three small stacks on left side of the table. On the right corner lay a larger tower which he was pulling from and separating. He licked his fingers, darting his eyes back and forth as he plucked another paper from the pile and flicked it onto the stacks. His movements were so wired, so manic that if Russ hadn't known better he'd have guessed Wayne was riding out some kind of cocaine bender.

"Maybe you're just too early," Russ said.

"Haha," Wayne said. "Very funny. Customers arrive in five minutes." He picked up one of the piles and tapped it straight against the countertop. "This is going to be your project this morning. I set up a small station for you in the back."

"Aren't I starting on the desk today?"

"When you're done with this."

"What is this?"

"Data," Wayne said. "We're crunching numbers. These are all of the forms from new members we've gotten in the past ten months." With the same frenzied motions, he scooped up the piles into his arms and began moving off to the back area behind the windows. "Grab that last stack there," he said, using his chin to point. He had the other piles heaped up into his biceps, teetering against his chest. One of the pieces blew free, sailing to the floor. "Crap!" he said, "get that one." He started talking again, yapping out instructions before Russ could even finish picking up the paper. Russ gathered it up and tried following his frantic pace across the floor. "I've been running special deals for first-time customers. Incentives," Wayne said. He was jogging now. "Everything from a chance at a free trip to the Bahamas to cash rewards to collector items like toy fishing boats."

"Fishing boats?" Russ said.

"There's been an influx of new parents in town. I don't know why. Grownups with toddlers, preteens and expendable income. Of course adults like them, too. We had one guy in here last month that asked for three. I guess he's been building a collection of rare and limited toys since childhood. Said he owned every Hess gas station truck ever produced since their inception in 1964. Never even takes them out of the packaging." They reached the folding table at the rear of the counters. Wayne crouched, unloading the papers onto it with a thud. "Your task is to organize these into different piles based on age, gender, reward and most importantly income level. I want to see which benefit is yielding the highest number of high rollers. We need more of them."

"Wellton has high rollers?" asked Russ.

"We need all of them that exist," Wayne said. He bent low over the first stack and began racing his finger over the pages. "Now, these lines here show the incentive that brought them on board. This column here shows their deposit and withdraw history. This is the gender line. Some of them are leaving that one blank these days. Lord only knows why. Over here you have frequency of visit. There's online check-in and there's..."

Russ couldn't keep up with all of the directions. Between Wayne's fluttering hands, his flashing eyes and his rapid speech, everything rushed together in the same blur. Part of the problem was Russ's complete failure to see the importance of the mission. What did it matter if females between thirty and forty preferred lavish beach vacations while males in their sixties leaned toward plastic boats? He didn't want to live or work in a world filled with useless toys and cheesy sunset posters. Meanwhile, the oceans were boiling, kids were hooked on opioids, and he still didn't know how to work the fucking bill shuffling machine.

Wayne was still spouting a steady gush of words. "Of course this will end up leading to a tangential issue of sorts. We'll need stiffer security for robberies. I'll go over that next week. We've got a new budget for armed guards now. I might even get to carry a gun for backup."

Russ's head was swirling. He'd completely lost any thread of coherence or connection. "So..." he started, but then he realized that he didn't know how to even begin explaining his level of confusion.

"Just get in there and crunch the numbers," Wayne said.

"Crunch them?" Russ said.

"Yeah," Wayne said. "Dig in, you know. Just get in there," he said. He made a swimming motion, like a breast stroke or somebody parting open a pair of heavy curtains. "Just get into the guts of it!"

Russ stared at Wayne, hoping to convey the true depth of his disorientation, but Wayne was not biting. "You'll be fine," he said. He rapped the top of a pile with his knuckles and smiled. "I have to go get the cash drawer ready. Do you want some coffee?"

"Yes," Russ said. "Definitely."

As soon as Wayne was gone the dread set in. Russ stared down at the sheets of paper until his eyes crossed and the letters on all of the pages faded into one big jumble of black ink. He may as well have been looking at the inner circuitry of a rocket engine or a book of recipes all written in Chinese. The feeling of helplessness grew until it overtook all of his senses. He was paralyzed with indecision and despair. There were eight more hours of work left, and Russ could envision no hope, no release from this malaise. Then the main entrance opened and the chimes rang out above the door and Russ was handed the momentary escape he was seeking. It was Natalie. She was even later than he was, and it was this shared indiscretion, along with her buoyant stride and her airy smile that lifted him out of his stupor. He had always loved a good partner in crime, and there was something about Natalie and her easy way of deflecting and reframing life's nagging struggles that had been cheering him a lot lately. It was not out of any romantic interest really, and Russ was grateful for that. It was more like she was his new spirit animal.

Before Russ knew what he was doing his arm was in the air and he was waving wildly in her direction, like someone flagging down a rescue helicopter on a deserted island. She transferred that breezy smile onto him and returned his wave, which offered him immense comfort, but she also seemed tentative about the extent of his animation. Russ lowered his elbow along with his level of zeal. His degree of embarrassment was heightened when he realized that there was someone coming in right behind her. She was a slender woman carrying an enormous suitcase and a large leather portfolio, both of which knocked against her knees as she labored to make her way through the vestibule. She had wooly, tousled bangs draped above a pair of bright yellow sunglasses, and her frayed blue jeans were cut short above the ankle. It was the type of bold style that intimidated with its amount of self-awareness and audacity. She was an artsy gal, Russ thought…

Darlene!

Russ had forgotten she was coming. This was the woman Natalie told him about, the one he should meet, she said, the one who was visiting on Friday, today. Russ locked his hands down at his sides and froze. Their eyes met only briefly as she banged her luggage through the employee entrance leading behind the counters. She was trapped there for a moment until Natalie came to help her maneuver inside.

"Wait," Natalie was saying, "so he's distracted? I thought therapists were supposed to be professional listeners.

"It's like he keeps grasping onto all the wrong details," Darlene said. "Last week he spent the entire session asking me about my cat."

"Your cat? What does that have to do with anything?"

"It was a shelter cat. I adopted it," Darlene said.

"So?" Natalie said.

"I guess he thought it meant something," Darlene said. "It's a needy cat, and I pretty much take care of it like it's my own flesh and blood."

They disappeared behind the door, and Russ looked up to see Wayne crossing the floor with two cups of coffee in his hands. Russ reached down and grabbed a hunk of paper from the tall stack. He placed it on top of the first pile. Then he returned and hastily, randomly divided the remaining sheets into two equal batches on the other piles. Wayne took a sip of coffee from his cup. A dribble leaked out and ran down his chin.

"Dang it," he said. "It's hot." he wiped the coffee away from his chin. "I guess that's a good thing. Hot coffee, right? Dang!" he said again. He handed the other cup to Russ. He took a step back and scanned the table. "You're done already?"

"Um," Russ said, "Yes?" He took an extra slow gulp from the cup, hoping to mask his trepidation behind the shape of it for as long as possible.

"Wow," Wayne said. "So did you find that the platinum bonus points were the biggest factor?"

"Well yeah, I mean..." He was still hiding behind the coffee.

"That's what I thought."

Wayne set his mug down on the corner of the table, again sloshing more liquid over the rim. This time it splashed his hand, streaming down between each finger and running onto the floor. "Ouch!" he shouted. He sucked the coffee off of his knuckles and groaned. He shook his hand out over the carpet, then peeled some of the paper back from the first stack and began reading.

"It seemed pretty even to me," Russ said. He thought he might be getting the hang of this business.

"Uh-huh," Wayne said, nodding down at the paper. "It doesn't surprise me because we also have a bunch of people who are interested in saving money on groceries and gas, but they're tired of those stupid punch cards, you know?"

"Um-hum," Russ said.

"You have to figure that everyone is looking for a little freebie these days. They have to scrimp because they're all trying to crack the next big invention. If you were to take all of the people under thirty-four and divide them into various categories, you'd find that about eighty percent of them are either trying to start their own business or looking to break into the technology sector, apps and stuff like that. They know that the gigs are drying up for them, so they figure if they can start their own company and gig someone else they can stay ahead of the curve. Trade up on a gig for a gig master. They have these things called incubators now…"

Russ had stopped listening again. All he could think about was Wayne's coffee stained hands and about how somebody might entrust those very fingers to handle a gun. Picturing the gun brought him back to the night of the murder. He'd never even really seen the gun. When Lang had asked him how he knew there was a gun for sure, he had only replied that there was something in his hand. There was a loud pop and then someone dead in the street. There was nothing else in the world that could create that effect. If a robber were to actually come into the bank he'd be forced to look at the thing, face the fact of its physical existence, encounter its designed purpose before it was even enacted and that seemed more than any person could bear.

"To be honest," Wayne continued, "if I could figure out some way to collect this type of data or a different set of data, and quantify it, you know… uh, use it to inform other selling points or drive other markets, I'd probably quit tomorrow. I wish I could cook up some scheme to pinpoint data that every business needs to thrive or modernize. The medical field is always looking. Mass marketing. Education! Education is so thirsty for data storage and metrics they'd pay almost anything. I could be a billionaire."

"Maybe you could use this project as a launching pad," Russ said.

"Yeah, maybe. I don't know," Wayne said, "I was just spitballing. I shouldn't have said anything. I like my job. Just dreaming. Anyway," Wayne said, clapping his hands together, "I'll look closer at this later. I think you're ready."

"Oh, I don't know about that," Russ said.

"Sure," Wayne said. "You're a smart guy. I knew that already. I mean, talk about a quick study. You've been here everyday, mostly on time, and you've been working hard. You've earned your shot."

"But I haven't learned everything," Russ said.

"I've taught you all of my tricks."

"Yeah, but I don't need tricks, I need -"

"Oh, everyone needs tricks. That's the good stuff. Don't worry. I'm the one who trained you. If you're concerned about having access to undercover secrets, don't be. You're good."

"No," Russ said. "It's not the secrets I'm worried about. It's the fundamentals."

"Then don't be worried at all. Tricks are a higher form of thinking, and if you've digested those, the fundamentals will fall into place. I've been thinking about downsizing our entire teller crew, paring down our service employees to focus more on projects like this one to maximize our return. We need program directors, copywriters. Our board and our stockholders don't care about how many small handshake deals or petty transactions we make. They want big numbers."

During the brief silence that followed, Wayne must have noticed the look of concern on Russ's face. "Oh, don't worry," he said. "I intend on keeping you and Natalie. No new hires though. The two of you can man the desk, so to speak, and also take on some marketing projects on the side. You can take turns. It'll be a nice career advancement for the two of you."

"Yeah, but aren't we known for having staff who take the time to give added attention at the booths here? Small town stuff, right. I mean, don't we get a lot of customers looking for extra care here?" Russ said. "Hasn't that been our bread and butter? Our motto is, 'People who care about your money as much as you do.'"

"Sure, of course, but they trust us to care about their money in a way that generates their highest return on investment. They may not say it out loud, but they don't want to be small town forever, or at least they wouldn't if they knew the other side. They don't really know how to care about their money like we do."

"I don't know how to care more than they care," Russ said. "Or care better than they do? I guess that's what I'm worried about."

"Look," Wayne said. "You're overthinking this. Let me do all the heavy lifting here, okay. Just get in there and do your best. I'll be here for backup if you need anything," Wayne said.

"You'll be right here," Russ said.

"I'll be nearby the whole time."

"Okay," Russ said.

"Okay," Wayne said. "That's the spirit. There's nobody here yet. Just sip some coffee and get yourself organized. Take your time. Take some deep breaths. Orient yourself. You'll be great."

Russ looked down at the counter in front of him and all its instruments of customer service. There was a computer monitor set to some sort of psychedelic screensaver. A series of twirling multi-colored loops arced across the screen, vanished out of sight and reappeared on the other side. A flexible microphone angled out from the center of the desktop like a plastic snake head. Various office supplies like paper clips and scissors sat inside wire baskets waiting to be called upon for some job Russ could not imagine. There was nothing to organize and everything at the same time. He moved a stapler from one side of the table to the other. When he finished a man was standing at the window in front of him. He was tall enough that his head was a good five inches above Russ's eye level. Russ was looking straight into his breast pocket which held a mass of loose paper, two pens and a highlighter. He took his hat off and as it passed down through Russ's line of vision it made him a little dizzy. It was an old fashioned hat, an olive green bowler with a red feather on the side. The man had a wiry mustache, red suspenders and a skinny chain leading from his front pocket to a belt loop somewhere in back. Between his gray whiskers and the musty tobacco smell, he could have been anywhere between fifty and one hundred and fifty years old. He may as well have been looking at JP Morgan himself.

"New checks," the man said. He had a gruff, gravelly voice as though his mustache was the thing doing his talking for him. He cleared his throat. There was a lot of congestion to cut through. It was possible he hadn't spoken in a very long time and needed to make room for it in his vocal chords.

"Okay," Russ said. "You need more checks. I think we can handle that." He turned around to find Wayne, and to his horror Wayne was nowhere to be seen. "I just need to check with my manager."

"Is there a problem?" the man asked.

"No, no problem at all. It's just that I'm new here, and I'm not sure how to... I don't know the best way to help you with this."

"It can't be hard."

"No, it can't be," Russ said. "If you'll just excuse me -"

The man cycled through a series of more throat clears, snorts and grunts. The sounds, it was clear, were meant to signal that he would wait but only for a minimum and disgruntled amount of time. Meanwhile, Russ was in a furious search for Wayne. It was a deranged sort of searching, the kind that had him checking for Wayne's presence under chairs and tables behind him.

"Could I speak to the manager?" the man said.

"That's what I'm trying to do now," Russ said.

"Do you even work here? I don't have time for this!" he shouted.

"Wayne!" Russ called. Wayne had appeared at the sound of the man's hollering. He had apparently gone to the restroom, and was now approaching with a quickened gait, mopping his hands dry on the pleats of his pants.

"Yes," Wayne said, hurrying around the counter. "Yes, sir. What can I help you with today?"

"You can help me by giving me some new blank checks. I guess your new fella here has never heard of checks before."

Wayne looked at Russ with disappointment, as though he'd told him a hundred times where to find blank checks for irate customers. "I don't recall," Russ said.

"It's no problem, sir," Wayne said, "but may I suggest that the process is actually faster and easier online."

"Christ!" the man said. "Oh, am I online?" He spun around, checking to see if he had accidentally tripped and fallen into some sort of internet vortex. "I'm not online, am I? It doesn't appear so. No, I'm *in* line! I'm in your god damned line right now!" He pounded the table so hard with his fist that Russ could feel it inside of him. The vibration started in his ears and rumbled down to the pit of his stomach. And then the images were back again, the gun smoke, the smack of the body hitting the pavement… Russ was surprised to realize his hands were up over his ears. Had he even been the one to put them there? It took everything he had not to collapse down onto one knee right there in the middle of the floor.

"Russ?" Wayne said. "What's wrong? Are you okay?"

"What is this? What is he doing?" the man asked.

"Just a minute," Wayne said. "Russ."

Russ's breathing was speeding up, growing loud and choppy.

"Hey, come on now," the man said. He spun around again and held his arms up, begging someone, anyone to notice the absurdity of what he was witnessing.

"Natalie!" Wayne called.

"Yes!" Natalie's voice came from three windows down. It was soothing and tender. Russ wished he could see her; he longed for the relief her appearance could bring.

"Take over here, please," Wayne said. "We'll be right back. Excuse us," he said.

Wayne took Russ by the elbow and led him around the bulletproof glass to the service exit. Russ could hear the man's muffled voice fading away. "This is the absolute last thing I have time for today," he said. He could hear Natalie's footsteps rushing over to cover for him. She'd come, without hesitation, bounding over with all of that generosity and kindness of hers just spilling out all over the place. Russ hated to be doing this to her.

Wayne was silent on their march across the carpet. When they reached the breakroom, he threw open the door and shut it fast behind them.

"Sit down," he said. He walked over to the cooler and filled a cup. The water burped and burbled inside the plastic jug. "Sit down," he said again. Russ sat on the loveseat against the wall. Wayne handed him the cup and Russ took a sip.

His breathing was still coming in gusts and his heart still raced, but being removed from the mustached man and all of the harsh lighting of the main floor helped. The water helped, too. He had to slow down his breaths just to swallow, and the more he drank the more his wheezing died down and returned to normal.

"What is going on?" Wayne asked.

Russ did not think he could explain this mixture of melancholy and terror churning inside of him. Wayne had never understood even his smallest thoughts or explanations about anything before. How could he possibly fathom this? Russ's eyes settled on something new on the counter along the wall. Some time between last night and this morning a fishbowl had appeared next to the microwave. It looked brand new. The glass was clean and clear and the base was already filled with a bed of pink pebbles.

Wayne sat down on the couch beside him. The seat was so small that their legs touched. It was a gesture so intimate that it made Russ shiver a bit. Wayne tugged his knee away, bracing it against the cushion by clamping his arm around it.

"Would it help if I shared something that was bothering me first?" Wayne asked.

Russ wasn't in good enough shape to speak yet, but he could nod. He wondered who had bought the fish tank and what kind of fish they would put in it. He loved looking at fish, especially the bettas with their bright feathery fins and shiny blue scales, but he hated taking care of them. People were always liking the idea of pretty things, but didn't want to put the time into keeping them that way. At least he was honest about it.

"Okay," Wayne said. He took a deep breath. "My dad is in the hospital." He paused, fiddled with his glasses. He took them off and rubbed the bridge of his nose. "He has a brain tumor. You may have noticed that I'm taking phone calls in private all the time, and I'm disappearing into the bathroom and stuff like that. I'm not handling it well. I'm not doing well."

Russ took one last big exhale and composed himself. "Shit. I'm sorry, man," he said. "I'm really sorry. I didn't know that."

"Yeah, I haven't told anyone. It took my dad almost a month for him to say anything, and now he's dying. It's awful. The worst part is that I didn't even notice, you know. I keep wondering if he was just waiting for me to notice on my own so that he wouldn't have to put himself out there and tell me himself. After he did tell me I finally saw the thing." He put his glasses back on. "The thing was actually like pushing on his skull in back. It was like blooming, I guess, growing. He pulled his hair back just a little bit and there was like this golf ball sized lump right there. I should have seen it, and now it's too late."

"No," Russ said, "That's not your fault. You can't make anyone talk about that shit. You didn't do anything. How could you possibly be looking for something like that? You couldn't. That's why people should be more open," Russ said. "That stuff is important for people to know, you know," he said. "That's how… They can help you."

"Yeah, so that's why I wanted to tell you. I don't want to pretend that it's not real anymore."

"Yeah, okay," Russ said. "Thank you." Maybe Wayne had bought the fish tank as a distraction. Taking care of a fish might take his mind off of things, make him feel better about not being able to care for his dad the way he wanted to. The fish bowl had a whole new meaning, and now he felt like an asshole for considering it such a trivial purchase.

"Yeah," Wayne said. He put his thumbnail in his teeth and bit down, then he took it out, looked at it, and put it back in again. "All right so... So now it's your turn," he grumbled. The thumbnail seemed like a small piece of remorse to be ruminated upon, like maybe he regretted saying the whole thing.

Russ nodded. He finished the rest of the water. He crushed the paper cup in his hand and clutched it there. "I saw someone get killed a few weeks ago," he said.

"Wait. You actually saw it?" Wayne said. He sat forward, put his elbows on his knees. "Oh, wow. Wow. My god. That must have been scary."

"It was horrifying."

"Crap," Wayne said, "Wow. I'm sorry. That explains a lot actually."

"Yeah," Russ said. The paper cup began disintegrating in his closed palm.

"Wait," Wayne said. "When? Who was it? Who got killed?"

"His name was Kirby."

"Kirby Baxter?"

"Yeah," Wayne said. "You heard about it? Well, I guess that's obvious. Nobody gets murdered in Wellton without the whole town knowing about it."

"Yeah, true, but believe it or not, I actually have a connection to the case," Wayne said.

"Really? How so?" The cup was turning to putty. Wayne uncurled his fingers and let it fall to the floor at his feet.

"I went to school with Kirby's aunt, Brianna. We went to Hanford together. It's a little community college near Fredericksburg. We're still tight, me and her." He started squirming around in his seat, itchy and agitated all of a sudden. "We just talked a few days ago. She can't get it off her mind. God, she's devastated."

"It's all so sad," Russ said.

"It's really sad," Wayne said. He shook his head. "People are so mean and cruel. You have no idea what they say."

"No, I have an idea. I know they are," Russ said.

"Yeah, but I mean you have no idea how many people said that he must have deserved it. They said he was hanging with the wrong crowd, doing the wrong things. Like he was asking for it. They said these things to her face, mind you. The audacity," he said. "It's unthinkable."

"He was a good kid."

"He was a great kid."

"People don't understand," Russ said.

"What crowd was he supposed to hang with?"

"Exactly."

"They got families up there at Valley View," Wayne said. "They have them way up there where they're so far away, so isolated… There's no real way of doing anything that's not marked by poverty or desolation or, or addiction. What are they supposed to do? Who's their crowd? What crowd?"

"Like they have some other place to be, a separate set of options. As if Gatsby and his band of socialites live just across the bay," Russ said. "And they have no escape. Generations of no escape. Mothers, fathers, grandparents."

"Great grandparents," Wayne said. "Great great grandparents. Lost, forgotten, pushed aside."

"They can't see a way out," Russ said. "They literally can't see it."

"And nobody even seems to care how they got up there in the first place. Where is it even? What is it? What is Valley View? It's not even a place, man, it's an idea," Wayne said. Russ had never heard him talk this way before. Something was coming over him. He didn't even look the same anymore. He looked weathered somehow, wisened. Maybe it was his dad that had opened things up inside of him. Maybe it was Kirby. "You hear it all the time. Every time a new crime or OD pops up it's like fodder for another sermon or something. And it's happening more and more these days."

"What else are they good for, right? What else is another dead kid among a crowd of dead-end kids?"

"That's their only way out. A casket being hauled down the hill. Or, or, a towney cop come to transport them to jail…"

"Past the billboard and out into the glare of news cameras and nosey neighbors along Main Street. Out with their frowning kids, teaching and learning lessons."

"And I go to their churches, Russ," he said. He put his head in his hand and kneaded the skin around his eyebrows.

"It's not easy, knowing what to do," Russ said. "We live in the lowlands, the world of the basin dwellers."

"And that's all anyone knows," Wayne said. "The tragedies. A Valley View tragedy equates to a moral victory down on Main Street. That's all anyone knows or thinks they know or what they want to know… Or what they *need* to know.... A Valley View life doesn't matter outside the parable of their demise. It's like they need them to fail so that we can seem like a little bit more of a success in comparison. It's sickening." Wayne said. "And nobody actually cares to know more."

"Yes," Russ said, "My God. I agree," he said. "We agree." And he was so overwhelmed with gratitude, so overtaken with the fact that they finally saw eye to eye on something, something so crucial, that he felt like he might cry. He was trying to hold it in, but when he looked at Wayne he saw that he had his glasses off again, and he was dabbing a tear away from his own cheek.

"It isn't fair," Wayne said. "Nothing is. None of it. Fuck," he said.

Russ couldn't hold it back any longer, and then they were both crying. Before either of them could fully engage in the weeping that needed to happen, they were both on their feet trying to end it before it got started. Wayne went back to the water cooler and poured another drink. Russ walked over and pulled some Kleenex out of a box and began wiping his nose and eyes. It was through these private but shared dances that they began to understand one another. Russ picked up his cup from the floor and crammed his tissue down inside it.

"Wayne," Russ said as he threw the cup away. "How do my eyes look?"

"Like you just stabbed hot daggers into them and twisted," Wayne said.

Russ laughed. "You look like shit, too!"

"I know," Wayne said. They both laughed together for a while until they tired themselves out. Laughter, it appeared, was the reverse side of tears, both outlets for untended emotions that had nowhere else to go but out. There was a thin line between the two, Russ thought. Afterward they helped one another straighten their ties and smooth out their shirts.

"What is the fish tank for?" Russ asked.

"Oh, Christ, I don't know," Wayne said. "It's for the customers, I guess. I was going to put it out by the entrance. Fish are supposed to symbolize prosperity. There's a pet store across the street from where my dad goes for his treatments. Yesterday, I don't know, I found myself drawn to the place. Guess I needed to look at something different, you know? I needed to think about something other than hospital beds and tubes and radiation... And... Well, as you can see I haven't gotten very far with the idea." Wayne laughed, dabbed his eyes and nose again with his sleeve. "It's stupid. I'll probably return it tomorrow."

"It's not stupid," Russ said. "I get it. Just the possibility of filling it up. It's something to look forward to. It gives you something different to think about."

"Yeah," Wayne said. "That's pretty much it. It's getting past the thinking part that's tough. The action part seems so hard."

"I know what you mean," Russ said. He looked at the empty tank. He couldn't decide if it was making things better or worse. Maybe he'd take it back for Wayne today after work. It might be best to just have it out of sight so he wouldn't be reminded of his inability to act, his inertia. Or maybe he'd buy some fish and fill it up for him. That would be a nice gesture. Most likely he wouldn't do anything. It felt good to think about doing it, though. "Can I take a smoke break?" Russ asked.

"Take two," Wayne said.

"Thanks," Russ said.

"Yeah," Wayne said. "Thank you."

Russ was just about to open the door and leave when Wayne called his name. "Don't tell anybody about my dad," he said. "I want to tell them myself."

"Of course. That's the only way it should be," Russ said.

Back out in the lobby things were quiet. There was one person over in the loan department talking to a guy named Garrett, one of the few other employees who still had a job to do worth saving. Russ had said no more than three words to Garret in the past two weeks. Russ wondered if he would be one of the guys on Wayne's firing line. A couple of people were in the vestibule using the ATM. The big man with the suspenders and mustache was gone. Russ knew for sure without looking. There's a certain way in which a man of that stature fills up a space with his presence so that when he has gone there is an unmistakable feeling of vacancy and purging. It's the same way a small yard feels after two enormous oak trees have been chopped down and hauled off or the way a neighborhood feels after a huge house has been demolished and steamrolled flat. You know they're gone without even looking, and that was good because Russ did not have the strength to look over and see Natalie right now. He needed to get out of there.

Russ took a seat on the curb and pulled his cigarettes out of his pocket. The sun was hidden behind a swath of gray clouds, but it was still humid and sticky. It was about two weeks before Thanksgiving and still a solid seventy-five degrees. It had rained at least five out of the last seven days. If you watched the weather reports these days, Russ had stopped in order to preserve whatever stitch of sanity he had left, you'd hear about how this autumn was both the hottest and wettest on record. Russ resented how his generation was doomed to think about armaggedon every fucking time they stepped outside their front door. There was no time or space for recovery anymore. You escaped one bout of dread only to be endlessly confronted with the calamity of uncontrollable weather patterns. This wasn't a catastrophe like the ones that had befallen previous generations. Wars and bigotry were formidable adversaries for sure, but this was different. You couldn't reason or negotiate with mother nature. There was no defeating this foe, no eloquent sermons or victory parades. This was bigger than human decency. Though the climate had been changed by humans, it had grown beyond their governance. It had enveloped and devoured all of humanity with its ruthless, indiscriminate fangs, and what was more frightening than that? Nothing.

"Would you be open to some company?"

Russ was so deep in thought that he didn't respond at first. "Huh?" he said, looking up to meet eyes with Darlene. She was smiling down at him, her brown eyes twinkling behind those dazzling yellow glasses. "Oh, why not? I think I could use some distraction," he said. She stepped carefully off the curb. She brushed her palms down the back of her jeans, ironing flat some phantom dress that didn't exist before wiggling down beside him. She sat close enough to assert her confidence but not so tight that it might startle him. As soon as she was situated and Russ could smell the faint scent of her herbal shampoo, he realized that this was the worst time for a pretty woman to be sitting next to him for the first time. Surely his eyes were still red, his cheeks still splotchy and his outfit a rumpled mess. He swept the sleeve of his shirt over his forehead and across his nostrils, still a bit damp with snot.

"Natalie told me you were a smoker. You don't see too many of your kind around these days. It's almost… quaint."

"Aw, yes," Russ said. "We're a dying breed."

"Literally," Darlene said.

"Why do I feel like you're about to ask for one, but you don't know how?"

"I might," she said. "I don't usually, but…"

"Keep telling yourself that," Russ said. He was still adrift in his thoughts, but this little foray was helping bring him out of it.

"Is it too soon to ask about what's distracting you?"

"Oh, hell yes," Russ said. "But it's not you. I mean, it's nothing you've done. I don't know," he trailed off. "There isn't anyone in the world who would want to hear about the distractions that consume me on a daily basis."

"Haha! Natalie told me you were funny," she said.

"I wish she hadn't done that," Russ said.

"Really? Why?"

"It's too much pressure. It makes me feel like I'm on stage or something, like a comedian. I don't want to feel like I have to tell jokes to an audience. I don't even have a set written. Aren't comedians supposed to have like a solid five minutes prepared or something like that? See, I don't have that. I can't handle those expectations."

Darlene laughed as though he had in fact just told a very funny joke. "You are hilarious!"

This was not an uncommon reaction for people to have when he was simply talking in what he considered to be a normal tone about regular things. Natalie, for example. She loved to laugh at everything he said as if he were Jim Gaffigan or something. He could never quite tell if the response was one he should be flattered or embarrassed by. Molly was one of the few people in his life, he had come to realize, who hadn't found him humorous even when he was trying to be. That was worse, Russ decided. He'd rather be thought of as a clown than be around someone who never cracked a smile even when something was funny.

Darlene was looking straight at him without an ounce of shyness or hesitation. It made Russ feel both guarded and emboldened at once. At the moment she was staring at his mouth and the cigarette that kept swaying in and out of his lips. She watched the smoke trail up above his head and drift away.

"So, do you want to bum a smoke?" Russ asked.

"Maybe," Darlene said, "but I don't think you are supposed to ask that way."

"What? What way?"

"I don't think it's politically correct to say 'bum' anymore."

"Oh, really," Russ said. "What is the appropriate way to talk about bumming these days."

"That's the thing. You aren't supposed to say bum at all anymore."

"What are we to call them?"

"Person without a permanent residence?" Darlene said.

"Okay," Russ said, "Would you like to 'person without a permanent residence' a smoke from me?"

"Hahahaha!" Natalie laughed. "You can't do that," she said. "You can't make me laugh about that."

"Why not?"

"Because I basically believe in the idea of using the language that people prefer. I'm for treating people with sensitivity and understanding."

"Oh, so am I," Russ said. "Without question. I would never call a homeless person a bum. Never. The thing is, we weren't talking about people without a residence or whatever at all. That's my only issue with political correctness. There's no allowance for context or proportionality."

"Natalie was so dead on about you. You are something else."

"I guess I just don't see the point in creating new names for things that were never really all that offensive or problematic in the first place."

"Maybe that's because you've never had the occasion to be offended. You've never felt like a description has been unjustly attributed to you that didn't fit your preferred image or personhood."

Russ took a long pull from his cigarette. He turned to exhale all of the smoke away from Darlene. When he turned back to face her he was wearing a large and conspicuous smile.

"What?" Darlene said, grinning. Russ could see how she and Natalie had become friends. They probably had never shared the same aesthetics, but as he had learned many times in life, yins needed yangs, and in the end a good sense of humor could overcome just about any amount of dissimilitude.

"Nothing," Russ said. "That was… that was sharp." There was no way to hide the enthusiasm he felt at having an exchange like that with a fetching woman who not only knew her shit but clearly savored the chance to dole it out. He pinched the cigarette in his mouth and dipped into his pack to get one for Darlene. She accepted it, and Russ leaned in to light it for her. Their arms brushed as Russ pulled away, and he felt a hot tingling pass from his elbow down into the gulf between his legs.

Darlene took a drag. She leaned back, planting one palm down on the concrete behind her. When she did this her knees parted just slightly and Russ's heart skipped. "Can I run something by you about an art project I've been working on?"

He couldn't respond fast enough. "I'd be insulted if you didn't," he said.

"I wouldn't normally do this, but you seem like a good audience."

"I'm more comfortable being the audience."

"Ah, that's right. The tables have turned. Okay, good. So, I did this portrait of sorts for my final capstone project. It's on a big white canvas, five feet by three feet." She put the cigarette in her lips and made a rectangle with her arms to illustrate the size. She squinted at it through the stream of smoke curling up around her eyes. Her arms were thin and tanned with just a touch of soft brown hair. "I painted this silhouette, more like an outline, of a woman. It takes up the whole space vertically, but on the sides I made a diagram."

"Like a doctor's chart?" Russ asked.

"Yes," she said.

"I'm intrigued."

"Right, so picture a doctor's diagram of a nude female silhouette. It's a pregnant woman with a noticeable bump. That's important. Up top where the brain would be is a cup filled with diet Pepsi. Through the middle, dangling like a spinal column, is a strand of pill boxes, like Tylenol and NyQuil and XYZAL. Around the vagina are things like a swordfish and raw eggs."

"That's quite a collage," Russ said.

"In a way. It's supposed to be illustrating all of the senseless and sensible things a woman is supposed to avoid during a time in her life when she is most vulnerable. My question is, is it too foolish? I mean, it's supposed to be a little foolish."

"I don't see the foolishness," Russ said.

"Well, I'm not all the way done. The feet. The feet are swollen, like two oafish balloons. Are you picturing this? Russ? You look like you're picturing it…"

Russ was indeed picturing it. He had a very clear image of the portrait she was painting. She had done a fine job of describing the features, and he was enjoying the process of tracing her depiction. However, he had also just been jarred from the daydream by a woman pumping gas across the street. It had taken a few second glances and some jolts of recollection, but he was certain now that it was Molly. Russ was now faced with the very real sight of a woman he had once loved and the drawing of a hypothetical woman outlined in his mind by another woman who he was already fantasizing about.

"I'm sorry," Russ said.

"What? It's no good. You don't like it. I haven't even finished explaining it," Darlene said. She sat up straight and ashed onto the pavement. Her eyes tried following Russ's line of sight. She put a hand up over her brow and strained forward, then she flopped back in defeat. Russ could see that she was already beginning to wither a bit, shrinking up into herself.

"No, no," Russ said. "I just..." Molly looked over at him then, and even though they must have been a hundred feet away or more, the glare of recognition was piercing. Russ observed as she cycled through a series of facial ticks and gestures, from a half-smile to a frown, from a suspended stance of shock to a jittery fleeing back inside her purple Chevy. The car, as it had always been, was washed and waxed, immaculate inside and out. She looked exactly the same, perhaps even more attractive in her short and summery skirt, and had he seen her a mere three minutes before this moment, his heart would have filled with longing. Now, knowing that she had witnessed him sitting here next to this enchanting woman, the blow was softened considerably.

"Hey!" Darlene said. "Are you still here? Hello? You can't do this to a girl. You're killing me."

Not only was the blow softened, but it was, to his great relief, removed altogether. Russ found that the pang he had initially felt was already dissipating and retreating from his consciousness. The bite that her presence could have produced was missing, like an electric fence with the power switched off.

"I'm so sorry," Russ said. "I was picturing it, truly."

"And?"

"And it seems lovely, really fascinating. I mean it." He had the impulse to reach over and grab her hand, but he knew that would be inappropriate. It was a bit staggering how close he felt to her already.

Meanwhile, Molly pulled away from the pump and accelerated out of the lot. She must have been laying on the gas extra hard because the bottom of her car scraped the ramp on the way out and made a loud grinding sound against the undercarriage. Maybe it was the noise that snapped him out of his daze or the bolstering realization that when her car disappeared so might all of his pining that had lingered too long.

"Okay, then what did I say?" Darlene asked.

"You were describing a diagram of a pregnant woman with various medical and nutritional objects tethered to her naked figure."

"And what were you looking at?"

"I was mostly trying to sort of, you know, mentally conjure the portrait you were describing." He mimed a circle above his head like a halo to show he was working on something up there. "I did get sidetracked, and I apologize. It's not important though. I don't want to focus on that. I want you to tell me more about your art."

She edged away from him and made a face like someone had just pushed her. "You are a weird dude," she said. She tossed her cigarette away into some bushes and put her elbows on her knees. Russ noted that she moved her leg back closer to his as she eased back into place. "You're lucky."

"Lucky and weird," Russ said. "I wouldn't argue with that, at least not at the moment."

"You're very lucky," she repeated, holding back a laugh. "I could just get up and walk away."

"Yeah, okay. I'm lucky. Okay, when you force me to admit it like that," he said, allowing another flirtatious smile. "Tell me more about your project."

"I'm calling it 'Lady Cop.' It's a comment on how women have been allowing men to police their bodies forever, especially when they are pregnant. It's supposed to be amusing but also arresting, you know? Is it thought provoking?"

"Well, I'm thinking about it. You have me thinking." He made a comical show of putting his hand up to his chin and stroking an imaginary beard.

She gave him a playful swat on the shoulder and gasped. "Stop it!" she said. "You are such a jerk!"

"I love it," Russ said. "It's provocative and subversive. Those are artsy words right?"

"Those are the most artsy words!" she exclaimed. "Okay, and now you are making me feel good about this. You're redeeming yourself. Say more. Keep going. I need this."

"I think it's timely. I know that men need to reckon with a model like that, and I think women could benefit from questioning their own inclinations, you know, like buying in, allowing men to control them like that."

Darlene blushed. She hunched forward and put her head down between her knees to hide her complexion. Russ let her hide. He finished his smoke and flicked it to the side. Her back was narrow and the bend that it made right before her hip bone, the perfect geometry of it, made him swallow hard.

She poked her head back up, draped a strand of shaggy brown hair behind her ear. "Are you going to tell me about what was distracting you back there?"

"Which time?"

"Oh my God! Both times! All of them!"

"So many distractions…"

"Now you're making it worse again."

"I could to tell you, but it depends," Russ said.

"On what?"

"On if you agree to see me again."

The door opened behind them, and Wayne appeared. He put one foot out on the sidewalk and peered around the frame. "Hey!" he said. "You coming back in or are you taking a vacation day?"

"This is no vacation," Russ said. He swung his arms out, referring to the parking lot stretched out before him.

"Very funny."

"I'm coming," Russ said. He stood up and straightened his tie. Darlene moved to stand as well, and once again he had to fight the urge to reach out and grab her hand.

Wayne vanished back inside and pulled the door shut.

"Maybe," Darlene said.

"I'll take that," Russ said.

They stood and stared at one another for a beat. Russ's chest felt tight and he found that he had to remind himself to breathe.

"You should go back before you get fired," Darlene said.

"Yeah, right."

She walked ahead of him and he held the door for her. The temperature had stayed the same and the clouds were just as dark and dismal as before. The sun had not turned black or fallen from the sky, and it was hard for Russ to remember the distraught feeling he'd had when he first stepped outside. This was what it must be like, he thought, the pleasant but numbing sensation of living in the present moment.

9

They laid together afterward, their naked bodies entwined on the tiny twin mattress. Had he known they were going to sleep together on the first night, he thought he might have ordered another bed, a larger one with a headboard and frame so that they weren't resting clear on the floor. But he knew that wasn't true. He'd only received one paycheck from the bank so far and that went directly to groceries and utility bills. If he had known this would happen, he also might have picked up the dirty laundry piled next to the hamper or vacuumed the carpet free of potato chips, dust motes and dried mud clots. The breeze from the rotating box-fan in the window ruffled the debris and skimmed across the sheets where Darlene hiked the quilt up closer to her neck.

Russ fished around beside the mattress and found his jeans. He stuck his hand inside the front pocket and located his pack of cigarettes. He plucked one out and then offered it over to Darlene. She accepted it, and placed one in her mouth. Russ lit hers first then did his own. He leaned back against the wall and inhaled.

"You smoke too much," Darlene said.

"Yeah, well you probably should have considered that before you agreed to go get pizza with me."

"Getting pizza," Darlene said. "Is that what the kids are calling it these days?"

Russ started to laugh but it quickly turned into a hacking cough that forced him to sit up and pound his chest. "Oh, man," he said.

"Seriously," Darlene said.

After work on Friday, Russ had asked Darlene if she wanted to go get some pizza later on. She said she was spending the night with Natalie but agreed to hang out Saturday instead. Natalie dropped her off at his apartment. The pizza place was close and because it was a warm night, the plan was that they'd walk over together. It was early, only about six o'clock, and he was still getting ready. Russ told her she could sit and watch some TV while he showered but because the place really only had two rooms, and because his toiletries were randomly scattered all over the house, they had to keep crossing paths. She asked him why his shaving cream was on the coffee table, and he had no answer. He couldn't remember why his razor was over by the stove or why his hairbrush was on the top shelf of his closet. As Russ traveled back and forth from the bathroom to the family room, they talked about politics, which was pretty much the least sensual topic anyone could take up. They were engaged in a deep conversation about how social media would be the biggest factor in the upcoming election, and about how Joe Biden would be too old to understand the battlefield, when Russ noticed that Darlene had slipped off her shoes and had pulled a pillow out from under the comforter. It wasn't like she was being seductive choosing the bed as her seat because the bed was the only spot to sit down in the whole place, but when Russ had to come back out of the bathroom for the fourth time to retrieve his deodorant, and Darlene was stretched out there with her legs crossed and her blouse half-undone, looking at him like she had something on her mind that wasn't going to go away unless they acted upon it, it just happened. It was almost as if he had planned it except there wasn't a chance in hell that he could have planned for a sexual encounter like the one they experienced if he had practiced and prepared for an entire month. He was simply, as Darlene had preordained, going through a spate of good luck.

"I have a frozen pizza we could make here," Russ said.

"Of course you do," Darlene said.

"What is that supposed to mean?"

"Oh let's see," she said, "a single bro in his mid-twenties with a frozen pizza on hand. What are the chances?"

"Hey," Russ said. "I'm not a bro."

"It doesn't mean what you think it does anymore," Darlene said.

"Aaaaaand we're back on the semantics of language," Russ said.

"Oh, come on. You love it," she said. She squirmed her leg over against his and nudged his shoulder.

"I totally do," he said, and all he had to do was turn his face a tad to the left and they were packed so tight together that their lips automatically touched. They shared a long and satisfying kiss. They could have sunk back into each other and gone in for round two, but he was still recovering from the first time, and he was hungry. He shimmied out of bed, grabbed his boxers from the floor and tugged them on. He almost left his shirt off, but he was still a bit self-conscious.

"It's got pepperoni," Russ said. "I hope that's okay." He opened the freezer and pulled it down. It was covered in thin shards of ice. He preheated the oven, plopped the pizza down on the counter and waited.

"What is that supposed to mean?" Darlene asked.

"I don't know. We bros don't have the sophisticated pallet to discern various lifestyle choices or dietary restrictions."

"Please. I eat meat like it's going out of style."

"That's good, because it actually is," Russ said.

"Shut up," Darlene said, and they laughed again. Laughing was so easy with her.

"Another hurtful stereotype revealed and destroyed," he said. He cracked the window and sat on the radiator coils. He blew the smoke out the open frame.

"Speaking of stereotypes," Darlene said.

There was some rustling going on under the sheets. When she reappeared her shirt and bra were both back on. The cigarette was still lit. She picked the conversation back up like it had never stopped. Such strange and beautiful magicians women were...

"Did you see that performance artists who posed as a conservative? He dressed up like a republican and went on Fox News?" she said.

"How does one dress up like a republican?"

"You pretty much just put on a red tie, comb your hair to the right and go on Sean Hannity."

"That'll do it," Russ said. "Sorry, continue."

"Dude was a hardcore socialist all the way. He went on and started talking about how he was going to push for higher minimum wage for unskilled workers, cheaper healthcare for large families and more affordable housing for low income citizens. He threw in something about reduced childcare and voila! I think he used the name Harold George."

"That's genius," Russ said.

"He said he was running for some bogus senate seat vacated in Omaha or some ridiculous thing like that..."

"Even better. He really went for it. I love it."

"Dude racked up 34,000 followers on Twitter before someone turned him in," Darlene said. She took one more drag from her smoke and then held it out for Russ to grab. He stood up and took it from her. He ran it under the sink faucet and threw it in the trash. "The commenters started out by saying, 'Real American with heart!' and, 'Libtard cupcakes won't know what to do with this thoroughbred,' stuff like that. They shared his interview all over the internet. Most of the conservatives were posting it to friends who supported the Democratic party, as a sort of, 'fuck you, you self-righeous, dick!'"

"Ha!" Russ said. He flung his smoke out the open window and shut it.

"Yeah, but when the conservatives found out it was just a hoax..."

"Oh, no. Holy shit. Watch out!" He opened the oven and slid the pizza inside.

"It was insane," Darlene said. "I remember one comment said something like, 'If I ever catch this faggot cunt, I'll rip his heart out through his anus!'"

"Jesus," Russ said. "I was going to say that the Dems got the last laugh, but that just sounds scary."

"I guess that's sort of the point, right? Here we all are walking around so close to agreeing and connecting, and a few useless labels and petty squabbles send us running for our guns and scalpel blades."

"Yikes..." Russ said. "That's visceral."

"It's just something to consider," Darlene said.

Russ sat back down on the radiator and stared out the window, It was past eight o'clock now and the final glimmers of sunlight had burned off into darkness. The alley was silent. It was the kind of quiet that a few nights earlier might have made Russ feel lonesome and tense but now seemed valuable.

Footsteps creaked overhead as someone walked across the floor in the apartment above.

"Are you going to tell me about what was distracting you yesterday," Darlene asked.

"I did say I would, didn't I?"

"You promised."

"I didn't officially promise," Russ said. "That's not exactly what I said."

"Here we go again," Darlene said.

Russ's cell phone rang somewhere under the covers piled on the floor.

"Saved by the bell," Russ said.

It took a while to unearth the phone. Russ's searching was half-hearted at first, but when he saw that the screen said "Daniel" he found that he was propelled into action.

"Hello!" Russ said, catching it on the last ring before voicemail.

"Are you okay?" Daniel said.

"Are you okay?" Russ said.

"Yeah," Daniel said, "I was just calling because I think I have one final idea that might work on James and Wesley."

The conversation did not last long. Daniel always had a way of getting straight to the point, never lingering on any notes of sentimentality or indecision. He had no time for soft emotions or social graces, and Russ, never being big on small talk, could appreciate that about him. What you could tell pretty quickly was that Daniel was a man who had seen himself through enough major turmoil in his life to know that minor hassles were a waste of time; a nice man who knew sometimes niceties could just get in the way. He was a big picture guy. Still, being a meticulous man as well, he had to layout the plan step by step. And there was the matter of convincing Russ to play along with his new and intricate role, as Daniel saw it. It wasn't much of a role, really. As usual he was mostly involved as a buffer and peacemaker, but it was the third time Daniel had asked him for a favor, and Russ could tell he was nervous. Russ would have said yes regardless, but he did ask for one condition. He wanted to bring along Richie and Darlene. Richie owed him one, and he had a feeling he might add some needed potency to the group's efforts. Darlene he just wanted along for the ride because he wasn't ready to part with her yet. Daniel agreed, and they set a time to meet at the house in the morning. He'd already arranged for James and Wesley to meet them there around nine o'clock. Russ hung up the phone. Darlene was looking at him like he'd just gotten done discussing a plot to rob a bank.

"What?" Russ said.

"That's what I want to know," she said. "Who was that?"

"It's a long story."

"You're stacking up quite a lot of stories to tell, mister" Darlene said.

"We'll have time," Russ said.

"Oh, really?"

"Yeah," he said.

Darlene made a show of sniffing the air. "You know the pizza is burning?"

"Oh, no, that's not burning. That just means it's done." Russ opened the oven door. He grabbed a dishrag on the counter and slid the pizza out onto the stovetop. "See," he said. "You start to know what smell means burnt and which one means perfection." He held the pizza up and tilted it toward her for display. "Pretty sweet, huh? Bubbly in the middle, lightly browned on the edges. It's a very old oven. You'll just have to get used to it."

"I see," Darlene said. "You're making an awful lot of assumptions here, you know that?"

"Well, when you're a bro who can make a frozen pizza like this, you can afford such luxuries."

"You are such a dork!" Darlene said.

In a momentary lapse of modesty, Darlene shot forward in bed and plucked one of her shoes off the floor. Dangling off the mattress, she pretended to throw the thing at him, nearly toppling onto the floor. She let out a joyous little giggle, as he just stood there for a second, grinning. And then, in a flight of giddiness, he allowed himself one phony, mischievous wink to top it all off, just because he could. Because he knew he had her, and he hadn't felt this good in a long time.

On the walk to the Holcomb house the next morning, Russ tried filling Darlene in on all of the details involving the fire and the ensuing refusal to sell the property to Teresa and Daniel. Richie had agreed to meet up with them at the apartment and he listened as Russ recounted the particulars. This wasn't the first time Russ had told Richie about the situation, but because he was now involved with it, because he was about to be a party to the case, he went into it with added depth and Richie listened with extra intent.

"And so, the inspector and Lang are in cahoots?" Richie said. He was having a hard time keeping up. For some reason his limp was particularly bad this morning. He kept having to walk a few steps then stop and drag his right foot back up to meet him. It was Darlene who noticed and slowed them down.

"Hold on," Darlene said. She didn't say anything, but instead motioned at Richie's leg so that only Russ, who had walked ahead several paces, could see. Richie picked up on the gesture without needing the full choreography. She'd only known him for five minutes and already they were communicating through telepathy.

"Thank you, Darlene," Richie said, huffing to keep up.

"Sorry," Russ said, "They have to be in cahoots. Why else would they keep following each other around and finishing each other's half-assed sentences?"

"Maybe they're in love," Darlene said.

"Not possible," Russ said. "They're too in love with themselves to notice anyone else."

"So, what are we doing right now?" Richie asked.

"Good question," Darlene said.

"You guys do realize that I am talking as fast as I can. We're walking, and I've been talking the entire time. I'm out of breath here," Russ said. "I'm getting to that. Give me a break."

"You're the one walking fifty miles an hour," Darlene said.

"Right?" Richie said.

"I hate both of you," Russ said.

"Okay, okay," Darlene said. "Go on."

"Daniel's idea, as he explained it on the phone, is that he and Teresa have prepared tamales and fried plantains, and they are bringing Tecates and limes over to try and woo James and Lang into seeing things their way."

"Do you think he has a chance?" Darlene asked.

"Daniel says nobody can resist Teresa's cooking, and he says that he hasn't turned on his charm yet, and he has faith in his abilities of persuasion." Nobody responded. Russ looked from Richie to Darlene, both of whom were starting to slow their walk at the exact same intervals. "What?" They came to a complete stop in the middle of the sidewalk. "Look, I don't think it will work either, but I have to try. I'm in too deep. I can't pull out now. What's the worst that could happen?"

"At least the weather looks like it will hold out," Richie said.

"For once," Russ said. "You never know anymore. We could have a fucking earthquake this afternoon for all we know."

"An earthquake? In Wellton?" Darlene said.

"He means it metaphorically, sorta. Russ is a bit of a doomsdayer when it comes to climate change," Richie said. "He thinks we're about ten seconds away from a natural disaster that is going to flatten all 8 billion of us at once. I'm not quite that extreme, but if I'm being honest, my figuring isn't that far behind his."

"That was one of the distractions," Russ said.

"What?" Darlene said.

"A distraction, one of them, from when we met. That was one of the things I was thinking about when you first came out and shared that smoke break with me at the bank."

"Oh," she said. "I see."

"You see how it's not the most airy of subjects. Not something you necessarily lead with in the old flirtation department."

"I wouldn't have cared," Darlene said. "I told you about my weird art project within the first five minutes."

"You're an artist?" Richie said. "You didn't tell me that, Russ."

"Jesus!" Russ said. "You've known each other for like twelve seconds now. I would have gotten there eventually. Christ, get off my nuts!"

"It's just that I have an art project that I'm working on related to the weather," Richie said.

"Really?" Darlene said. "Let's hear it!"

"Okay, best friends forever. Can we at least walk and talk at the same time? We don't have all day!"

"This guy," Richie said, scoffing and pointing with his thumb.

"Geeeeeeeez," Darlene droned.

"Fucking A..." Russ sighed.

They started walking again, but not as fast as Russ would have preferred. He tried to slow down, but the rate was too tedious, and so he sped ahead. "It's a video montage of incoming thunderstorms in real time..." Richie was saying.

For the next couple of minutes Russ walked a few strides up while Richie and Darlene bonded over their mutual appreciation for abstract expressionism. The weather was still warm for mid-November, but nothing crazy. The clouds were a mixture of blue and gray, like someone had pumped the sky full of smoke. There was enough of a nip in the air that Russ had on a zip-up hoodie and Darlene had on a denim jacket with a wool collar. Richie, perhaps for intimidation purposes, was wearing nothing more than a pair of ripped jeans and a plain white T-shirt. At first Russ was surprised he hadn't brought along his white Adidas jacket for this ride but, as usual, Richie come up with a better idea. Russ wondered if Darlene thought differently of him after seeing Richie. She must have known that Richie was the muscle in the friendship, and she must have understood that Richie was called into action because Russ wasn't certain he could handle the situation on his own. The relationship was brand new, and the slightest crack in his armor could be a threat to his chances of convincing her of his masculinity. But then he thought about how Darlene didn't seem like the type of woman who would get hung up on something like machismo, and he started realizing that this was the exact kind of paranoid delusions that always got him in trouble in the past, and then luckily, before he could spiral any further, Richie came up behind him and tapped on the shoulder. When Russ turned around he saw Darlene a couple steps behind him, staring down at her phone.

"Psssst!" Richie said. "Yo, you did good," he whispered. "She's a Twinkle Eye for sure."

It made Russ happy to hear him use that term. This was a nickname he gave to people he really liked. Richie had a philosophy, another drunken one of course, that the two most important qualities a person could have were an openness to adventure and the intelligence to see life as the absurd spectacle it all was. He said that when those two attributes were in harmony, when they collided, he could tell because the person had a certain type of quick and knowing smile and a flash of recognition, which he called "receptivity," in their gaze. In other words, people who were open to a wide range of ideas and up for just about anything were Twinkle Eyes.

"Thanks, buddy," Russ said. "That means a lot to me." They shared a brief elbow nudge of affection, which was about as tender as the two of them got, before Richie started applying a noogie to the top of Russ's head and he pulled away.

Teresa and Dan came into view up ahead. They sat in two of the six lawn chairs placed in a half circle facing the curb. All of the chairs were rainbow striped and straight from the Walmart down the street. Some of them still had the tags attached to the headrest. The last time Russ was at Walmart he saw them in the camping section, displayed next to a bunch of erected tents suspended from the ceiling and a popup camper cutout made of cardboard. They were the kind of chairs that sat low to the ground so that Daniel and Teresa's butts were sagging onto the grass beneath their weight. The burnt house in the background made the scene look like some artist's rendering, a stark comment on the futility of modern materialism. As Russ got closer he could see that Daniel and Teresa were both wearing identical sweatshirts with "Pennsylvania" printed across the middle with rows of leafy trees in various states of color change. Teresa's was extra large and baggy. Something about them looked cleaner and more polished for some reason. Daniel was freshly shaven and Teresa's hair had an added shimmer about it. Russ noticed she had also put some lipstick on and applied some kind of blue shading around her eyelids. Everything about this first appearance made Russ feel nauseous with despair.

"Hey!" Russ said. He cheerfully greeted them as they both struggled to wobble their way out of the low chairs. It took Teresa longer than Daniel. Teresa might have toppled right over onto her head if Daniel and Russ hadn't both reached out and grabbed hold of her elbows.

Daniel and Teresa both gave Russ a warm and hearty hug. "And this must be Richie and Darlene." Darlene had sped up when she saw them stand and was able to rush and meet Daniel's handshake as he extended his arm. As soon as Daniel let go, Teresa was right on top of her. She went right in for a hug. Darlene was so caught off guard that she couldn't get her arms out in time, and so Teresa's embrace pinned her arms down at her side and made her look like a pencil. Richie was lagging behind but scrambling to catch up.

"Howdy," Richie said. He was out of breath and hobbling badly, but he was trucking as fast as he could. Russ reached out to support him, but he brushed his hand away. "I'm fine. Daniel," he said, smiling. He reached out and gave his hand a vigorous shake. When Teresa approached him he was prepared. This time he was the one who caught her a bit unaware. "Teresa!" He wrapped his arms around her and bore into her. For a brief moment it looked as if her neck might get crushed by his shoulder, but then he let go and stepped back. "It is so nice to meet you two," he said. "Russ talks fondly about you all the time."

"That's nice," Daniel said. "He's been a real friend through all of this."

"Please, have some tamale," Teresa said. There was a cooler next to her chair. When she opened it Russ could see three large baggies filled with steaming tamales in golden husks. Below them he spotted the red and gold cans of Tecate beer. "Here," she said, but when she leaned forward she almost fell over again.

Daniel steadied her by placing one arm on her back and guiding her hips back up to standing position.

"I will get them for you," Daniel said. "Please, please, sit down."

As Daniel pulled out the tamales and began distributing them, Teresa, Darlene and Russ took a seat in the row. For some reason Richie wouldn't sit in the remaining chair. He was standing off to the side, quietly nodding his head and counting seats. He leaned heavily on his good foot.

"What are you doing?" Russ asked.

"I'm going to stand," he said.

"No," Russ said. "Why?"

"There aren't enough chairs," Richie said. "It's totally fine. I'm not complaining."

"There's an extra chair right here," Darlene said, tapping the seat next to her.

"No, see we have to wait for James and Wesley," Richie said. "There are six total chairs, but there will be seven of us here today. It's more important that they have a place to sit down."

"I'll stand," Russ said. "Here."

"No," Richie said. "No, I'm fine. Seriously."

"Come on, Richie," Russ said. He bent closer to him and said in a hushed voice, "I know your leg is hurting you. Just sit down please."

"No!" Richie said. "I'm not sitting down. I'm good right here."

"You're not good," Darlene said. Darlene stood then too and came over to help Russ. "You're being stubborn."

"Ack, you guys are making such a fuss over nothing," Richie said.

"Yeah well, so be it. Let us fuss," Russ said. "Now sit your ass down."

Russ and Darlene each took a shoulder and walked him over to a chair. At first he was going down easy, but then he thought twice about it and started to put up a fight. It was like trying to cram an angry bull into its pen, but finally they were able to wrangle him into place.

"God damn it," Richie said as he slammed down onto the fabric seat. They were all lucky his big ass didn't pop straight through to the ground.

"Eat your tamale," Russ said.

Darlene unwrapped hers and took a bite. "These are amazing, Teresa."

"Thank you!" she said. "It's a family recipe."

"I've heard these take a lot of time and care to prepare," Russ said.

"That's no lie," Teresa said.

"How did you get the dough to be so spongy on the outside?" Darlene asked.

"Oh, honey, that would take a long time to explain. It's mostly the lard and the broth and the baking soda, but if you want we can talk about it later."

Everyone was seated now. The order, from left to right, went Daniel, then Teresa, Darlene and then Richie. That left the two chairs on the far right open for James and Lang, which was good because right then they were pulling up to the curb across the street.

"Is that them?" Richie said, nodding over at the red pickup with huge tires and two small men inside.

"Yep," Russ said. "Can I get one of those beers, please?" Russ asked.

"Sure," Daniel said. He reached into the cooler and pulled one out. He popped the top open and carried it halfway to Russ who was coming to meet him. After that Daniel sat back down and started handing two more Tecates down the line.

"Look at these two, chumming it up," Richie said, eyeing Wesley and James as they made their way across the street. "Two little midgets coming to a tallest man competition." Darlene reached over and whacked him across the chest.

"Ouch!" Richie said. He looked up at Russ who took a sip of his beer and shrugged.

They came sauntering across the street, happily, the way people do when they feel they have nothing left to prove. James came dressed in his standard fleece and flannel woodsman getup. Wesley was walking straighter and taller in his civilian clothes than Russ had ever seen him before. Maybe it was the breezy flip flops he wore on his feet or perhaps it was the absence of a nightstick, holster and badge to weigh him down.

Daniel stood and welcomed them while everyone else stayed put. Russ made a gesture like a hat tip, only it looked more like a salute since he wasn't wearing any hat. The introductions were sparse and clipped, not because Russ or Daniel wanted to keep things impersonal, but because Richie and Darlene did. They both sat with their heads down and eyes averted throughout the greetings. The only time either looked up was when their names were called or when their relationships to Russ were explained.

"Howdy everyone," James said.

Darlene must have detected something off about the way James was standing over her, because she looked up again in time to catch him leering down at her. As Darlene raised her head, James was finishing his head-to-toe appraisal of her body with his eager eyes. His mouth had become involved in the examination too. There was lip licking as he rested his gaze in the center of Darlene's chest. Darlene did not waver. She kept her eyes locked on his, lying in wait, until he glanced up and met her glare. James clamped his mouth shut and swallowed. He backed away in a hurry and fled in the opposite direction. Darlene held her scowl a few more seconds to be sure he was through, then popped her can open and took a sip.

"These ours?" Wesley said, motioning toward the open chairs.

"Yes," Daniel said, "have a seat."

There was some shifting and bumping about as Daniel fished inside the cooler for beers and tamales. He got out paper plates and napkins. Each person passed the items down one by one until Wesley received his at the end of the line. There was a lot of pleasantries exchanged, mostly from James and Wesley. A few "excuse mes" and "pardons" with some "these look great" and "nothing like a nice cold one on a fall afternoon." Everyone else kept quiet, except Teresa who did her best to make small talk by telling them about the different varieties of tamale filling and asking about their holiday plans. Richie and Darlene stayed exceptionally silent and sullen. Russ worried they were being too foreboding, but maybe it was all part of their plan. Had they somehow worked out a covert plan together without telling anyone?

Following the bustle, a hush settled over the group. Russ wondered who would speak first. He felt obligated to be the one to say something if nobody else did. That would be part of his role, he assumed. Was he the only one thinking of these meetings in terms of roles and performances?

"We have two different kinds," Daniel said. "We got green chili and pork."

Everyone said they'd love one of each. Russ watched as James came inches away from chomping into one with the husk still on. Wesley caught him a second before, elbowing him in the hand and holding up his peeled one for reference. James caught on, but still bit into it gingerly with both hands like he expected some scalding liquid to come shooting out the other end.

"There are more if you'd like," Teresa said. "I make a few dozen each time. Arturo's favorite are the sweet ones with strawberries inside, but I didn't feel it was right for this occasion."

"Well, they are delicious," Wesley said. "Whatever the occasion. I'll take it."

For a moment, the seven of them all sitting around, eating together on lawn chairs and sipping some brewskis, it was like they were old friends. To the general observer walking past, it might have even looked like they were some kind of blended family out for a redneck picnic. Russ hoped someone did happen by and give them the old double or triple take. It made him laugh to picture their faces, trying to figure something out that couldn't be figured in the way they were used to thinking.

"Tasty," James said. He peeled a piece of pork from his chin and slurped up the juices. "Who is Arturo?"

"That's our nephew," Daniel said. "Don't you remember? He's the one who is going to college at Dickinson. In Carlisle." He leaned forward so he could scan both of their faces. "No?" he said.

"Yes," Wesley said. "I remember. James remembers, too. It's just… He's taken a lot of bumps to the head in his days. Right, James?"

"True," he said.

A few houses away a group of boys raced their bikes down a hill in the alleyway. The alley was bracketed on both sides by old apartment complexes with high brick walls. It was like riding down a tunnel with no roof. At the bottom of the alley was a speed hump. The idea was to peddle as fast as you could down the hill and then hit the bump full speed. The further the rider sailed the more badass he was. It was called a "Bump Battle." One of the kids played lookout at the bottom to check for traffic on the main road while the others prepared for their plummet at the top. Russ remembered, as a kid, how hard it was to overcome your terror and go charging down the hill. All of your faith was in the hands of another twelve-year-old boy who just wanted to see how far you could fly. Brushes with death were a rite of passage in Wellton. "Let's go!" the lookout boy yelled. He had a nest of wild blonde hair, a bike with bent handlebars and an ace bandage wrapped around his left elbow.

"We go back to El Paso in two days," Teresa said. "We need to secure a property. We need a new home so we can be close to Arturo. He's a bright kid, tough, but he needs family nearby. He can become the first person in his family to graduate, but he needs help."

"That's why we're prepared to raise our offer," Daniel said. "We brought you here to share our drinks, break some bread with us. We come to you with a pleading heart. We need you, *te necesitamos.*"

Wesley looked at James and James stopped eating mid-bite. A spell of bungling silence ensued as Wesley slid his plate under his chair and licked his fingers clean. "Look," he said, using the napkin to finish up his fingers, "Let me stop you right there. We appreciate all of this, we really do, but James and I had another talk on the way over here, and there's just no way to – "

"Two hundred thousand," Daniel said.

James turned sharply on Wesley. Russ saw him inch his foot across the grass until his leg nudged Wesley's knee. Russ himself could not believe what he was hearing.

"Right, well, be that as it may, we still can't sell," Wesley said.

"We? You can't sell? You?" Daniel asked.

"Um, no, well, James." Wesley said. "James, you explain."

"All right," James said. He took another loud gulp from his beer and cleared his throat. He put the beer on the ground beside him. "What I just found out is that there is another problem with the overall stability and uh, molecularity of the soil."

"What is it?" Teresa asked.

"Well, so soil under a foundation can only be so many parts dirt and so many parts ash," James said.

"You already told us this," Teresa said.

Richie made a snorting sound in the back of his throat. He shimmied his way up higher on his chair and reached into his side pocket for a cigarette. “Horse shit,” he mumbled under his breath.

As Richie made a move to place the cigarette in his mouth and set it aflame, a commotion broke out at the far left side of the row. Daniel reached over and flicked Teresa on the knee. Teresa responded by pulling her chair back from the line. Darlene looked over at Teresa who was cradling her tummy and edging farther away. Darlene gasped and whacked Richie’s cigarette out of his hand seconds before he brought the lighter to it.

“I have asthma,” Darlene said. She reached behind her and grabbed the leg of Teresa’s chair. Slowly, Teresa slid her chair back into the row. Russ watched as Teresa smoothed the fabric down around her sweatshirt and let her hands fall away from her stomach.

“Yo!” Richie said.

Darlene snapped her head around at Richie. Next, solely with the curvature of her neck and head and the arch of her eyes, she was able to communicate the seriousness of the situation. Richie followed her brows as she raised them, and then discretely lowered them, along with her neck and chin, toward Teresa’s belly. Russ watched the whole thing come together like a finely tuned dance number. Richie tilted his head back and opened his mouth. He brought his head forward lazily, like the slowest head nod in the world, and by the time his head was level and his mouth was shut, he understood everything. Teresa was pregnant.

“I don’t understand,” Daniel said, striking the conversation back up before anyone got too suspicious.

“It’s the soooooil,” James said, talking extra slowly in case it was the English language that had gotten in the way. “The moooolecules, need to be consiiiiiistent - “

"He heard what you said," Russ said.

"Yeah, the words were clear, just not the meaning or the reasoning. There's a malfunction," Richie said.

An exuberant whooping came from the boys in the alley. Another one had gone hurtling into death's path and lived to tell about it. They'd remember this forever. For as long as they all lived, there might never be a better call for celebration.

"Okay, okay," Wesley said. "I'm not sure I like where this is going."

"What?" Daniel said. "Where what is? What is the problem?"

"I don't know," Wesley said. "That's the problem. I got the lot of you over here squirming and jumping around like your butts are on fire, and then we have people raising their voices over a matter that is already a done deal."

"The matter isn't even a matter," Richie said. "There is no matter."

"You already told us about this," Daniel said. "We've been through this before."

"Yes, but there is additional reasoning now," Wesley said. "Go on, James."

"Yeah, um," James said. "See, it turns out there are different codes for different building plans. Business versus residential that is."

"For example?" Daniel asked.

"Well, for example," James said, "The standards for commercial real estate (in terms of ash percentages) are lower than that for family homes."

"There are a couple of retail developers looking at the lot already," Wesley said.

"I don't believe it," Daniel said. "How can this be? It's impossible."

"What are the businesses?" Teresa asked.

"A Hallmark store, I think was one of them," Wesley said. "What else was there, James?"

"An H & R Block, maybe," James said. "Wasn't there something about an Army recruitment center?"

"Jesus Christ!" Richie shouted.

"How can this be?" Daniel said. And the look on his face mirrored the confusion held in that simple question.

"We work so hard," Teresa said. "We've done everything right."

"We're trying to look out for you," Wesley said. "It's dangerous."

"But it's cool to put some accountants and military officers on the fucking soil?" Richie wanted to know.

"It's not the same," James said. "Residential properties are different. You have little kids, you've got grandparents, families eating dinner together on Christmas..."

"And grandchildren going off to war," Darlene huffed. "And the IRS robbing people blind."

"We don't care about the soil!" Daniel yelled, losing his patience for the first time.

"So you want a house built on a mass of sinking land?" Wesley said. "You want something set on quicksand?"

"Oh come on!" Richie said. "Quicksand? Quicksand! Remember when we were kids and everyone was scared that if they went too far into the woods or if they snooped around some old guy's property, they'd step in some quicksand and get swallowed up by the earth? We may as well have been worried about a piano falling on our fucking heads! We're not kids anymore, god damn it!"

"Hey!" Wesley said. "Hold on!"

Russ rushed over and put a hand on Richie's shoulder to keep him in his seat.

"I'm not going anywhere," Richie said.

James got to his feet and then Wesley shot up beside him.

"No!" Wesley said. He put a hand in the center of James's chest. He turned his whole body to face the house. "No. Hold on. Wait. Shhhhh," he said. "Do you hear that?

When all the voices were silent save the alley boys galvanized cheering, they each heard a sound coming from the house. It sounded like a cat meowing. It was a mournful cry, high pitched and drawn out at long, bleating intervals. Once you heard it, it was surprising it had taken so long for them to notice. It was like the siren on an ambulance.

Wesley stood with his ear cocked toward the house for another second and then took off running. One might guess his wife or child was trapped inside a fresh inferno the way he ran. Clods of dirt and grass kicked up beneath his tromping feet. With flip flops flopping under heel and knees pumping the air, he soared. He was fast for his size, loping strides that seemed to out pace his puny chicken legs. When he reached the house, he tore the door open and bolted inside. In a flash he dodged right then left and then vanished up the side staircase.

It happened too fast for anyone to have any natural reaction. Teresa stood and Daniel came up with her. He put his arms around her shoulders and hugged her close to him. Darlene turned nothing but her head. The rest of her body stayed planted in the lawn chair. Richie remained stationed, staring out at the street, sipping his beer and chewing his tamale. Russ was watching James, and James had no idea what to do. He looked at the house, then over at Russ, then back at the house again. He started to say something, but seemed too dumbstruck to do so.

"I'll be back," James said. He put his hands in the pockets of his flannel jacket and ambled toward the house. He walked in a daze, the way a man might walk through a hospital parking lot after just being told of his terminal diagnosis. Before he was even halfway there, Wesley came barreling back out of the house with something white and furry cradled in his arms. He came charging right at James. James, thinking he was being passed the animal, opened his arms to receive it, but Wesley lowered his shoulder and trudged right past him.

"Oh my God," Wesley said. "Look at this. Do you see this? Can you even believe it?"

Wesley unfurled his arms and held the cat out for everyone to see. It was a dusty almost beige colored cat; medium-sized with a few orange splotches on its paws and belly. Aside from its constant yowling and a small scab over its right eye, it looked to be fine.

"This is the cat that was lost in the fire," Wesley said. James came dawdling back to the group as dazed as he had left it. "Do you see this, James? It's a miracle!"

For a brief moment, they all looked upon this new specimen like a revelation handed down from high. James came close to Wesley and peered inside his arms. One by one they all gathered a bit closer to have a look. There was an ornery, ungrateful streak in it. Any moment, the flared claws implied, it could squirm free of Wesley's grasp and strike. Wesley yanked the cat away as though they might either contaminate it or learn too much, it was hard to say.

"Wasn't it a kitten?" Russ asked.

"What?" Wesley said. "So?"

"So…" Russ said, "that's a cat."

"It's been almost a month," Wesley said. "Kittens turn into cats."

"Yeah, a month," Russ said. "How long can a cat live without food or water?"

"Well, he must have been foraging," Wesley said, "He's a good scavenger. That's clear."

"I thought it was a gray one," Richie said.

"Where did you hear that?" Wesley asked.

"Read it in the newspaper," Richie said.

"You weren't reading the right newspaper," Wesley said.

"They publishing something different in one of the other Wellton County conglomerates?" Richie asked.

"Just back off, okay!" Wesley said. "Have a freaking heart! Not one of you has a soft spot for a cuddly creature like this? An animal that's been abandoned, left for dead?"

They all stood and looked at Wesley with his sooty cat and his darting eyes. They listened to the cat wail and claw at his shirt to get free. Nobody said anything.

"I grew up with cats my whole life," he added. "They need a good home."

Still there was no response. He took the bottom of his shirt and folded it up over the cat's bottom like a diaper. Its eyes were the only things not covered in ash. The color was so blue against the surrounding mottled gray fur, it made the poor thing look possessed.

"You're all a bunch of callous sons of bitches," Wesley said. "Let's go, James!" he said.

"Where are we going?" James said.

"Wait!" Teresa said. "You can't go yet. We still have plantains."

"There's more beer," Daniel said.

"Let's go!" Wesley said. He swung his hip over and banged it into James's side. "Come on!"

"Ouch!" James said. "What… where are we going?"

"To the god damned veterinarian hospital to take care of this poor thing like any normal folks would do under these circumstances." Wesley pivoted and marched off toward James's truck. "Let's go!"

James hesitated for a second. He was rubbing his side where he had been hit and contemplating what the hell was happening so fast. It didn't seem like an emergency, but he couldn't stand around with the agitated crew that surrounded him any longer, and so he headed off after Wesley with a new limp and a reluctant spirit.

Nobody quite knew what to do. It seemed like someone should stop them, but then Daniel and Teresa had already said all they could, and it didn't seem like anything else was going to change Wesley's mind. Maybe that's why Richie decided to take a different approach.

"You're a coward!" Richie hollered. He cupped his hands over his mouth and walked to the edge of the property line.

"Open the door," Wesley barked. "James! Get the engine running."

As Richie unleashed his fury on James and Wesley, Darlene and Russ turned their efforts toward Daniel and Teresa. Teresa had her head buried in Daniel's chest. Daniel watched as Richie continued to fire insults across the street. His lips quivered with desire to pile on, but he was past the stage of anger. If he started yelling now, he would not be able to stop. Words would only propel him toward physical assault, and that would not benefit Arturo or Teresa.

"That cat is a mirror!" Richie went on. "You're carrying your own hairy, misplaced soul! That love could be given to humans, you know. That should be the Flores family in your arms. In your heart. You fascist fuck!" He took a few steps onto the street, but halted before he hit the traffic.

Russ made his way over to Daniel and Teresa. He paused in front of them and waited for something, any words of solace to come. Darlene moved in close at his side.

"You don't have to say anything," Daniel said. "You tried. That's all we could have asked for. More than what we could ask for."

"I wish I could have done more," Russ said.

Teresa picked her head up from Daniel's breast. There were tears in her eyes. "I won't forget you." She looked over at Darlene and smiled. "Or your friends. You're good people."

"Arturo is going to make it," Russ said. "If he has even half the fight in him that you guys have, he's going to graduate with flying colors."

Teresa nodded. She wiped a tear away from one eye. The trail left a bluish black streak down the side of her cheek.

"You love that stupid cat more than you love the United States of America!" Richie shouted. This brought a smile to Teresa's face. They all smiled, and shared a little laugh.

Russ began worrying that the neighborhood was going to hear all of the commotion and come flooding out of their houses, but so far the only people who seemed to be paying any mind at all were the handful of roughnecks kicking around over in the alleyway. Russ saw one of them flap his arms up over his head and then wave some of his buddies over to come see what was going on. In a few seconds, three more kids, in their ripped jeans and trucker hats with the long hair curling out the back, came romping over and chose a seat for the event. Some of them balanced on their bike seats and leaned against a wall. One of them pulled a skateboard out from somewhere and sat on top, crouching forward with his elbows on his knees the way teens sometimes do when they're watching the best part of a bad movie.

"We should probably get him," Russ said

Teresa nodded. Daniel reached his hand out to shake, and Russ took it.

"You two are going to be okay, too," Darlene said. "I know I don't know you really at all, but I can just tell. Both of you are going to find a way…" she trailed off, then turned her gaze on Teresa's pregnant stomach. "Well, all three of you."

Teresa reached her hand out and grabbed Darlene's wrist. "Thank you," she whispered. They shared a brief nod of gratitude and then embraced. Teresa released Darlene and then wrapped Russ in a short but intense hug that made Russ feel like he was going to cry again.

"Owen Cummings!" Richie shouted. This one did get a reaction from Wesley. He halted halfway inside the truck. One leg hung outside the passenger door. The cat was struggling to break free. "Yeah! Yeah!" Richie said. "You heard that one, huh?"

Russ's spine went slack. Hearing Owen's name crumpled him up a bit. His gut cranked tight. He braced for the nausea but did not feel the same queasiness he once felt at any mention of the case. There was a gurgling but no eruption, and his body wrenched sideways, recalibrating for the lack of ejection. Darlene noticed his twitching. He tucked his chin down toward his shoulder and clamped his teeth shut. Darlene steadied him with one hand on his damp back. "What's wrong?" she asked. "Are you okay?"

"Ask about Owen Cummings!" Richie yelled. "Or have you ignorant bastards already called off your hunt? I bet you have! Not important enough for a guy like you, Lang? Huh? You need a cat murder to get you going, huh? What have you got to say for yourself?"

Russ knew that the only thing that could make it all go away was if James and Wesley left. He was able to hold his head up enough to see Wesley close his door and give James the signal to drive off, a whirling finger twirl and a whistle, like a homerun signal in baseball. The engine revved and in an instant Russ felt the contractions dissipate. He was able to straighten up and breathe.

"I'm okay," Russ said. "I'm fine." He put his hand on Darlene's shoulder. The amount of perspiration that had been released from his pores in such a short period of time was alarming. It slipped down the back of his neck and vanished below the elastic of his underwear. All of his clothing felt matted and slick against his skin.

"We should go get Richie," Darlene said. She rubbed her palm over Russ's back and felt his muscles loosen.

"Yeah," said Russ. He took another deep breath. He mopped his sweaty hands down the front of his pants, then faced Daniel and Teresa again. "Good luck," he said one last time as they tuned to go fetch Richie.

The truck had already pulled away from the curb and was a block down the road, but Richie was still going.

"You're the type of ass holes that make the rest of us Americans look like inhumane monsters!"

"Richie," Russ said. "That's enough. That's plenty." He put a hand on his shoulder and tried easing him back on the sidewalk.

"Take your feline fetish back where it came from. Get out of our country!"

"Okay, Richie," Russ said. "That's good."

Darlene's phone rang and she answered it. Russ managed to wrangle Richie over and get him to sit down on the edge of the curb. He was breathing as though he'd just been in a boxing match. It was like he'd been shadow boxing, sparring with himself for the past five minutes.

"He cares more about cats," Richie said.

"I know," Russ said. "I know. There's nothing you can do. You tried. You said your piece."

"They think they found something, but they didn't find shit," Richie said. "I'm not wrong."

"You're not wrong," Russ said. "You're looking for different things. You've got too much to say, and they don't want to take the time. You're giving them fucking poetry," Russ said. "They don't know what to do with that. Save it."

"Okay," Darlene said. She held her phone up and shook it at them. "That was Natalie. She wants us all to go have drinks tonight at some place called Clancy's?"

Russ laughed. "Ha! Oh man, Clancy's. At least we know Wayne won't be there."

"What?" Darlene said.

"What are you talking about, dude?" Richie said.

"Nothing, nothing. Sounds good to me. We should beware of diving birds though!"

"What are you even trying to say right now?" Darlene asked.

"Nothing. I'll tell you later."

"Here we go again," Darlene said. "We're up to like five untold stories now that I'll never hear the background for." She walked over and sat down next to Russ on the curb.

"Wait," Russ said. "Tomorrow is Monday. We have work."

Darlene whisked a hand up to her forehead and snapped it back down like a salute. "No, sir," she said. "Tomorrow is Veterans' Day."

"Oh, yeah," he said. "Riiiight. So that's what all the flags are for." He looked up and down the street. Many houses (at least half of them) had a big American one either waving from a post in their front yards or a little one sticking out the top of a mailbox. One of the houses, maybe five or six down, had a flag so large in the driveway that its billowing fabric blocked nearly every window in their home. No way anybody could see a damn thing. Blinded by the red, white and blue. There was something poetic about that, Russ thought. He couldn't tell if Darlene had picked up on the sarcasm he'd used in his comment about the flags. The flags had always been there. Nobody needed an occasion to show off their patriotism in Wellton. "God bless the troops," he said.

"Haha," Darlene said. "Oh, come on. You don't even believe in God. You told me that much on the first night we spent together."

"Romantic, huh?" Darlene laughed. "I don't even really believe in America."

"So you're just being blasphemous for the sake of being blasphemous then?" she asked.

"No, I do believe in troops," Russ said. "I support troops."

"Well, and now you're going to have even more of them around. A bunch of rabble-rousers signing up for service at the fucking recruitment office right behind you," Darlene said.

They both turned around for one last look at the Holcomb place. It didn't look so ominous or profound anymore, but more just lonely and rejected. Now that Russ knew it wasn't going to be a home for the Flores family as he had hoped, there was no big aura around it, sort of like an old antique everyone once thought was valuable but later found out was worthless. Russ understood how this appraisal made things less upsetting for him and more painful for Daniel and Teresa, but he didn't know what else to do about it. That was exactly what The Man did to a guy who dared to seek rectitude. He ground him down until he was so weary he couldn't squirm his way back out from under his god damn boot heel anymore.

"It's not their fault," Russ mumbled. "The machine needs feeding." It wasn't even clear if the words had come out at all or just stuck in his head. He didn't even know if he wanted to be heard anymore or if he wanted to be left alone. He was exhausted. This must have been what people meant when they used the phrase "dog tired." That was a common saying around Wellton, but Russ never knew what it felt like until now.

"Hey," Darlene said after a while. She yanked a few weeds out from between the sidewalk. "Were you really not going to go out tonight just because it's Monday tomorrow? I haven't known you that long, but you don't strike me as the type of guy who would be scared away by the prospect of a school night."

Russ laughed. He looked from Richie to Darlene and then back at Richie again. Richie arched one eyebrow. He raised the corner of his mouth and cocked his head to the side. "Shiiiiiiiiiit," he drawled.

"We'll never tell," Russ said.

Darlene laughed. "That's what I thought."

Russ put his arm around Richie's shoulder. "That sounds good, doesn't it? Kick back some beers. Blow off some steam? It'll be good for you."

Richie nodded. "Yeah, okay. I guess." He picked a small stone up from the street. He heaved and grunted as he hauled himself up onto his feet. He shook the stone in his hand as he turned to look at Daniel and Teresa over by the chairs. They were going from seat to seat, collecting beer cans and empty tamale bags. Richie reared back and threw the stone as far and as hard as he could into the abandoned house. It made a clunking sound as it struck the empty window near the roofline and then rattled a few more times as it settled down to the bottom floor.

One of the boys in the alley saw the gesture and responded the only way a young and mischievous kid knows how. "Fuck yeah!" he hollered. "Rock and roll!"

Richie raised his fingers up like a fork and put his tongue out. "Hell yeah!" he yelled back. It was the first time he'd smiled since they first met up in the morning. But his demeanor changed from one of hellraiser to good Samaritan when he looked up at Daniel and Teresa who were woefully cleaning up their belongings. This was the difference between twelve-year-old Richie and Russ and the guys who stood before them now. Russ couldn't help wondering what would become of those wayward yokels. He couldn't stop himself from loving them somehow, seeing himself and Richie and the whole wretched but formative town right there in their filthy little faces.

Teresa walked circles around the perimeter, picking up scraps of wrapper while Daniel folded up chairs and stacked them in his arms. "We should help them," Richie said.

"Yeah," said Darlene. "We should."

"For sure," said Russ. "We'll be right over."

Richie hobbled toward Daniel and Teresa. Russ put his arm around Darlene. "Thanks for coming along for this," he said.

"I'm glad I did," she said.

They hugged for a while and then Darlene gave him a little peck on the cheek. "I should spend this afternoon with Natalie before we meet up later."

"Yeah, that's cool," Russ said. He stood first, then reached down and helped Darlene up to her feet. "I need to just unwind for a minute anyway," he said. "Maybe I'll take a bath. I feel like I've been trying to relax for weeks now, and I just can't seem to…" he paused to breathe. He hadn't told Darlene the biggest secret of all yet. Kirby Baxter's murder was an imposing obstacle that stood in their way and Darlene didn't even know it existed. It was staggering to think about, but he knew somehow they'd make it through even that harrowing tale. "I need to allow myself, you know, to like... lower myself into it."

Darlene grabbed his hand and they walked together toward the chairs. She had her head down, watching her shoes as they scuffed across the grass. She must have been trying to figure out what it was he had just said, what all the codes and silences meant, but Russ knew there was no way to explain it now. He hadn't explained himself well at all. How could he? She could have asked him again what he was talking about, added another new story to the list of veiled ones to be revealed later, but she let it go this time instead. "Do what you have to do," she said, scraping some loose soil around with the toe of her shoe.

Richie was helping stuff the paper plates into a garbage bag. Darlene and Russ grabbed a few bags from the box on the ground and began tossing trash into them. "I saw the way Mr. Rolland ogled you like a piece of meat," he said.

"Oh, yeah. Ugh," Darlene said.

"You handled that like a pro. I mean, I was proud of you. That dick looked at you like I wasn't even just standing right there."

"You mean *like I* wasn't right there."

"Yeah," said Russ. "Right. Now that you say it that way." They dragged their bags across the lawn toward a few plates that had drifted away on the breeze.

"Don't worry about me," Darlene said, taking on a mocking tone, "just a floating sack of lady parts over here."

Russ laughed. "That must suck," he said. "I'm sorry. That's Wellton for you," he said, shaking his head. "Good old Wellton."

"Well," Darlene said. "I mean, yeah, but, you get used to that shit." They were just about to branch off in different directions, but Darlene reached out and caught his hand. She squeezed it extra tight and tugged. Russ halted, jerking back in her direction, and when he tumbled toward her she was right there, looking him straight in the eyes. "It's pretty much the same anywhere you go," she said.

Russ thought that sounded pretty true, for the most part. Maybe later he'd have something to say back to her about the idea, push her on it a little bit, have a friendly battle of wits. But he liked the way she said it and the way it was still lingering there in the air between them before she let go of him, both his eyes and his hand, and so he just nodded and smiled.

They spread out. Russ scavenging the roadside, Darlene picking her way toward the house. God, he was so happy to have found someone around Wellton he could match up with intellectually. But there would be plenty of time to enjoy their already familiar dynamic, Russ was certain of that. Right now they had to help Teresa and Daniel. They might be there awhile. How long does it take to clean up after all of someone's discarded pleas for mercy have withered and gone away? He could get buried in a thought like that...

Darlene stopped tidying abruptly. Every part of her body went stiff and straight, one hand paused over her open trash bag. There was a look on her face like maybe she was remembering something terrible, like maybe she had left a cigarette burning in one of the ashtrays before they left the apartment. Russ approached her with caution, circling in on her slowly, from an angle of least harm, the way one might attempt to awaken a sleepwalker. All of a sudden he was acutely aware of how little he knew about her and any hidden darkness she may be harboring. Perhaps she had flashbacks the way he did. It could be anything. As he got closer, her expression softened. Her hand started moving again, releasing the trash and reaching out to grab his elbow. She pulled him gently, almost artfully to the side and whispered something into his ear.

"Would now be a bad time to mention that I'm worried my cat isn't getting enough food while I'm gone?" she said. "Back in New York." Russ didn't say anything right away. The nutrition of her cat wasn't at all what he'd expected and the incongruity of it threw him a bit. A smile etched its way across his lips, and he shook it away. He watched as Daniel packed more garbage into a bursting trash bag and walked it to over to Richie who hoisted it up over his shoulder and made his way for the dumpster behind the property.

"Only the worst time ever," Russ said as they both fought back their swelling, mirthful grins. They did it privately and with consideration, so that anybody who may have looked over might have thought they were hugging instead of laughing into one another's shoulders. And once more, they were smiling in the midst of suffering together, thumbing their noses at life's agonizing absurdities. And really, Russ thought, is there anything more important than finding someone with which to do that?

"Hey!" One of the alley-kids yelled. He'd moved closer, astray from the pack, and now he stood only a dozen yards away or so. Russ and Darlene peeked up from their embrace to see a scrawny boy with a peach-fuzz mustache and double eyebrow piercings. His bare arms were covered in small peeling Band-Aids. He cupped a hand around the side of his ashen mouth, one blood stained bandage dangling from his elbow, and barked, "get a room!"

About the Author

SIMON A. SMITH teaches English and debate to high school students. He holds a BA in creative writing and an MAT in secondary education. His stories have appeared in many journals and media outlets, including *Hobart, PANK, Whiskey Island* and Chicago Public Radio. He is the author of two novels, *Son of Soothsayer* and *Wellton County Hunters: Book One of The Search Team Trilogy.* He lives in Chicago with his wife and son.